"*I really don't know what I have to do to make you approve of me, Justin.*"

Justin moved so his face was in the shadows and Lucy couldn't read his expression. "Just the one thing you won't do."

For the life of her, Lucy couldn't stem the images that flooded her mind, of lying in his arms and being made love to. "But then I might not approve of myself...."

LINDSAY ARMSTRONG was born in South Africa but now lives in Australia with her New Zealand-born husband and their five children. They have lived in nearly every state of Australia and tried their hand at some unusual—for them—occupations, such as farming and horse training, all grist to the mill for a writer! Lindsay started writing romances when their youngest child began school and she was left feeling at loose ends. She is still doing it and loving it.

Books by Lindsay Armstrong

HARLEQUIN PRESENTS
1874—DANGEROUS DECEIVER
1925—MARRIED FOR REAL

LINDSAY ARMSTRONG

When Enemies Marry...

Harlequin Books

TORONTO • NEW YORK • LONDON
AMSTERDAM • PARIS • SYDNEY • HAMBURG
STOCKHOLM • ATHENS • TOKYO • MILAN
MADRID • WARSAW • BUDAPEST • AUCKLAND

ISBN 0-373-11946-1

WHEN ENEMIES MARRY...

First North American Publication 1998.

This edition published by arrangement with Harlequin Books S.A.

® and TM are trademarks of the publisher. Trademarks indicated with ® are registered in the United States Patent and Trademark Office, the Canadian Trade Marks Office and in other countries.

Printed in U.S.A.

CHAPTER ONE

'JUSTIN, this is unbelievable; there's a photographer—oh, sorry, I didn't realise you were with someone.'

Lucinda Waite paused on the threshold of her husband's study, then swept in, continuing, 'But it's only you, Sasha—well, you and someone else. How do you do?' she added politely to the third party in the study. 'I'm Justin's wife Lucinda, but most people call me Lucy. Who are you?' she enquired, extending her hand graciously.

'Robert Lang,' the third party murmured, rising hastily and taking the extended hand. 'How do you do, Mrs Waite?' He was about twenty-three and looked both embarrassed and slightly dazed.

'Not very well, thank you, Mr Lang,' Lucy Waite replied with a grimace. 'My privacy is being invaded—and I can't help feeling you might be responsible for it all.'

Robert Lang blinked beneath a clear blue gaze and made a mental note that registered some surprise. They *were* the colour of deep blue velvety pansies, her eyes, and her skin had the texture of cream rosebuds while her hair, caught back carelessly, was the colour of ripe wheat. Now, now, he cautioned himself, letting his gaze drift over the rest of Lucinda Waite, it can't be all perfection. Short legs possibly, out of proportion with the rest of her, or hippy and pear-shaped, *thick* legs—no, his eyes widened, talk about legs, they were sensational...

'You're staring, Mr Lang,' Sasha Pearson said all but inaudibly and not quite kindly. She was an elegant redhead in her early thirties but whether she was family hadn't been made clear.

But Robert Lang, despite his youth, was not without charm and ingenuity. 'I sure am,' he conceded boyishly. 'In point of fact, I'm quite bowled over. I don't think I've ever seen anyone as lovely as you, Mrs Waite—er—if you'll forgive me for saying so, sir!' He turned deferentially to Justin Waite still sitting behind his desk, not altogether in a further demonstration of his charm but because, to his mind, Justin Waite was not the kind of man one gave offence to and possibly least of all in the matter of his stunningly beautiful, flawless, twenty-year-old-if-she-were-a-day wife.

'You're forgiven, Mr Lang,' Justin Waite said. 'My wife has been having that effect on people since she was in her cradle.' He moved in his chair and stood up, revealing most of the over six foot, lean, muscled length of him that, coupled with rather hard grey eyes and a look of worldliness and experience, had kindled Robert Lang's wariness in the first place. 'My wife has also,' he went on coolly, 'been leading people up the garden path for almost as long.'

Lang's eyes widened and jerked to Lucinda. But, far from any expression of outrage, she merely smiled faintly, and murmured, 'What have I done now, Justin?'

'Invaded your own privacy, my dear, from what I can gather. Did you or did you not write to a certain publication and invite them up here to do a story on the place, and on you?'

'Yes, I did—so that's who you are!' Lucy said to Lang with a glorious smile. 'But you didn't let me know you were coming. I thought you must be one of those maverick journalists who turn up from time to time and make my life a misery.'

'Lucy, that happened once and has never been repeated,' Justin Waite said in the kind of voice that caused Robert Lang some trepidation, although it didn't seem to have any effect on his wife.

'And the reason you didn't know he was coming, Lucy,' Sasha Pearson—where *did* she fit in? Robert wondered—rose and picked up a letter from the desk, 'is because while Justin and I were away you didn't bother to open any mail although you assured me you would.'

'That's right,' Robert Lang said eagerly. 'I did write and suggest today if it would suit you.'

'Oh, dear,' Lucy Waite said regretfully. 'You really should have waited for a reply, Mr Lang, but now I know who you are, we might as well go ahead. I've got nothing else on. By the way, you are indispensable, Sasha, aren't you? Forgive me for ever doubting it! I'll just go and get changed.'

'You'll do no such thing, Lucy.'

'Justin,' Lucy protested. 'Why not?'

Blue eyes stared into hard grey ones and, despite only mild protest registering in Lucy Waite's expression, the atmosphere was suddenly electric and Robert Lang found himself, to his amazement, wondering what went on behind locked doors between Justin Waite and his wife. Did he beat her or did he throw her down on the bed and make punishing love to her...

'Because I say so, Lucy,' Justin Waite said with sudden detachment as he looked away from his wife thereby seeming to cut the electric current between them. 'Go back to your horses, my dear, and I will apologise for this misunderstanding.'

Lucy Waite shrugged. 'Whatever you say, Justin,' she murmured. 'Do forgive me, Mr Lang,' she added. 'I haven't been married very long, you see, so I'm not altogether familiar with the *rules*, I guess, but I——'

'Lucy——'

'Just going, Justin. Bye!' She strolled out with a wave.

'I gather,' Justin Waite said across the dinner table, to his wife, 'that today's events were more shots in the war you promised me the day you married me, Lucy.'

Lucy Waite smoothed down the skirt of the clinging, long-sleeved black dress with a heart-shaped neckline that she'd changed into for dinner and picked up her soup spoon. She'd also tucked a creamy gardenia into the hair that was lying loose and rippling on her shoulders. 'You gather right, Justin.'

'It wasn't much of a shot.'

Lucy sipped her soup then grinned. 'As a matter of fact I thought it quite got you off the bit for a moment, Justin.' She changed her expression to one of severity and mimicked, ' "My wife has been leading people up the garden path from the cradle." But yes, it would have been better if it had come off,' she conceded. 'You do so hate publicity, don't you, Justin?'

'I can't believe you really enjoy it,' he commented drily.

Lucy wrinkled her nose. 'It was only a rural paper. I thought it was rather tasteful to choose a rural paper instead of a national daily. And all I'd planned to do was show them the house and some of...*our* treasures, and all your improvements to the property. It would have been quite a scoop for that young man, don't you think? Something about the Waites in a newspaper, even just a rural one. You've probably blighted his career, Justin, and he was rather sweet, really.'

'I haven't blighted his career at all, but he does understand now that my wife is off limits so you might as well forget him, Lucy. And any other young man who takes your fancy.'

Lucy laughed and pushed away her soup. 'You perceive me quaking in my shoes, Justin,' she murmured. 'Still, all may not be lost,' she mused. 'There's got to be at least one person out there now who's thinking that the Waites of Dalkeith and Riverbend have a very strange marriage.'

'On the contrary, there could be at least one person out there who is actually thinking that Lucinda Waite is a spoilt brat and deserves a good lesson.'

'From my experience of young men, Justin, they don't generally have those thoughts about me. It's only your generation—at least, you're the only one of your generation I have to go on, and I have to tell you that if you mean what I think you mean——'

'That you deserve to be put over someone's knee and ceremonially spanked?' he broke in lazily.

'How picturesque.' For the first time a little glint of anger lit Lucy's eyes. 'I have to tell you I should probably get so angry I'd even be capable of taking a pot-shot at *you*. Don't forget I'm an excellent shot and I would know exactly how to inconvenience you considerably without doing a lot of harm—and make it all look like an accident anyway.'

'That wasn't what I had in mind, Lucy,' he drawled, and reached for the decanter to pour himself some wine.

'How brave you are,' she retorted.

'What I had in mind—were I so minded,' he continued, holding his wine glass up to the light meditatively, 'was a lesson of another kind. Such as——' he put the glass down gently and their eyes locked '—removing your dress from your delectable body, uncovering your breasts and the rest of you and making love to you until you're—shall we say, in a much more amenable frame of mind? I have this theory on women,' he went on, idly inspecting the pulse that had started to beat rather erratically at the base of Lucy's throat. 'That without regular, satisfying sex they become fractious and troublesome, and in your case in particular, dear Lucy, that what you really need is a couple of kids to keep you out of mischief.'

It took Lucy several moments to gather enough composure to be able to speak, moments that were made worse for her because her tall, satanic husband did not relax his leisurely scrutiny of her in the slightest and then had the gall to pour her a glass of wine and push it towards her with a faintly amused twist of his lips.

In the end, as she sipped the golden liquid, it was he who spoke first. 'You don't agree?'

'I think,' Lucy said carefully, 'that it's a pity you didn't live in a different era, a bygone era for example, when women were treated like chattels and it was accepted practice to generalise about them as if they were so many...sheep. As if they had no minds, only instincts.'

'Then tell me this—you've ordered the course of this marriage so far; how happy has it made you?'

'You've gone along with it,' she said tautly.

'Were you secretly hoping I'd do something as uncouth and as—*exciting* as taking you against your will after you made your dramatic declaration on our wedding-night?'

Lucy gasped. 'Only minutes ago *you* were talking about... you *were* talking about...'

'Something quite different, Lucy,' he said.

'I can't see it, personally.' She looked at him defiantly.

'I was talking about finding out what your will really is in this matter,' he said and his teeth glinted in a sudden grin. 'Don't look so worried, I'm not going to do it. Not tonight, at least. But I do make the point that to a certain extent you've given me yourself as a hostage in this ridiculous war, Lucy, and perhaps you should bear it in mind the next time you decide to fire any shots. Would you care to dish up the casserole or shall I?'

Lucy put down her napkin and stood up. The silver casserole was on a hot plate on the sideboard. 'I will,' she said, but didn't move immediately. 'Justin, you gave me very little choice about marrying you. You made it very plain that I could lose everything I possessed, not the least my home, where I've lived all my *life*, if I didn't marry you. You put it to me that we could fight each other for years over Dalkeith and that you *would* fight for it although it was more or less all I had, while you'd inherited Riverbend and made yourself a huge fortune on top of it——'

'That's debatable——'

'Don't interrupt,' she commanded. 'But since you have, it was never my fault that our fathers were foolish enough to own this place in partnership and then even more foolish to fall out with each other and leave us to inherit this mess——'

'Lucy, the cold, hard facts of the matter are a little different. Because Riverbend and Dalkeith are adjoining properties and because our fathers were friends, when your father got into financial difficulties, *my* father offered to inject some money into the place and accept a partnership in return—a *silent* partnership,' he said significantly. And waited while Lucy tried to look unaffected but failed. He went on, 'What broke up the friendship, despite this concession to your father's ego, despite trying to help save Dalkeith from going under the hammer, was that your father persisted in believing that Australia could ride on the back of its sheep forever and fought every suggestion my father ever made for diversification away from growing wool.'

Lucy bit her lip. 'I didn't know all that,' she said bravely, however.

'No, but that wasn't my fault,' he retorted impatiently. 'It was his fault that you didn't know, his fault that you were allowed to queen it over all and sundry as Lucinda Wainright of Dalkeith and never suspect you'd have to share this place with anyone, let alone with *me*, whom your father had given you the impression you shouldn't want to know any more anyway. Although——' his eyes glinted '—there were times when you didn't mind knowing me, Lucy.'

She coloured faintly but said with spirit, 'If you're referring to the days when I was barely out of rompers and didn't know better than to follow you around whenever you were here——'

'As a matter of fact I'm not referring to those days,' he said softly—and said no more.

She blushed properly this time, which made her angrier. 'If this is your revenge for——' She stopped abruptly.

'It isn't,' he answered equably. 'Not against you, anyway.'

'Then tell me this, Justin: what *was* your motivation for coming to see me only a fortnight after my father's funeral and telling me that the only sensible course for us to pursue was to get married?'

'Ah, well, my better nature did slip a bit then, I have to confess. You were so proud. I could also visualise the complications that might arise if someone else married you or got you pregnant before we'd sorted it all out. You have to agree, Lucy, that you left a trail of broken hearts around the district—it was really only a matter of time before you—er—fell. But of course, there was also the way you'd grown up, five foot six of sheer perfection, a bobby-dazzler in fact,' he said with a shrug. 'It occurred to me that not only would I not mind being married to you, but, since we had such a lot in common——' his eyes drifted around the beautiful room '—it would simplify matters considerably.'

'I'm only surprised you don't have another theory,' Lucy said through her teeth. 'That wives can be schooled and trained like horses. Or is that still to come?'

'Provided you get them young enough, it could be a possibility, even though you were so spoilt and indulged by your father,' he said indifferently and shrugged again. 'Lucy, how much longer do we have to wait to eat? We've had all this out before. And you were the one,' he said with sudden impatience, 'who accepted my proposal. Which to my mind, if we're really discussing moral superiority, puts us on a par. Although you mentioned earlier that I threatened you with something like poverty. In fact I offered to buy you out, and that would have been a long way from poverty, my dear.'

'But I didn't want to be bought out. I decided to fight in the only way I could think of for my birthright, Justin. My great-grandparents happen to be buried here, and my mother and now my father, I love every acre of Dalkeith and sometimes, when you love something enough, you're prepared to go to extraordinary lengths to preserve it. Besides which, it occurred to *me*,' she said softly, 'that you'd find it not considerably simpler but much more difficult to dispossess a wife, Justin.'

'A wife, yes, Lucy,' he said. 'But there are certain things you have to do to become a true wife.'

'It's only your word against mine—ah,' she said to herself. 'So that's why you haven't forced me to go to bed with you! You're keeping your options open, aren't you, Justin? But while an annulment on the grounds of non-consummation may entitle me to less of your property, it is only your word against mine.'

He lay back in his chair and watched her. 'Would you lie about something like that, Lucy?'

'Where you're concerned, I might. Don't forget, I have to put up with your mistress parading herself around my home—who knows what flights of fancy the mere fact of that might prompt in me—where is Sasha, by the way?'

'She's gone back to Riverbend and she's not my mistress.'

'Then she's dying to be your mistress.'

'She happens to be an employee, my private assistant in charge of the stud at Riverbend, as you very well know, and she's extremely good at her job, that's all; what makes you think she has...the ambition you're accusing her of?'

Lucy turned to the sideboard at last. 'You'd probably have to be a woman to understand that. But I would have thought even you could see the sort of censorious way she treats me.'

'There are times when you lay yourself open to that, Lucy.'

Lucy heaped a fragrant portion of lemon chicken on to a plate, and some steaming, fluffy rice, and laughed. 'Perhaps I do. But she does so obviously hold this conviction that you were mad to marry me whatever else she is or isn't, you see. On the subject of mistresses, by the way...' She turned and carried his plate over to him, not unaware that his gaze was following every move she made, then went back for her own. 'At thirty, you must have had some, probably dozens. You're successful, you're good-looking when you're not being critical and superior—did none of them prompt you to think of marriage for all the right reasons?' She sat down and helped herself to salad then courteously handed the crystal bowl to him. 'Take Joanna Madden, for example,' she added pointedly. 'I'm sure a lot of people thought that was a *fait accompli*.'

'So did I—once upon a time,' she said musingly after a while when she thought he wasn't going to answer.

'What happened? Did she have nothing as enticing as the other half of Dalkeith to offer you?'

'She—had her reasons.'

'You don't seem particularly perturbed,' Lucy said witheringly.

He smiled fleetingly. 'One lives and learns, I guess. Lucy,' he said after a pause, 'considering our feelings on the subject of Dalkeith—and while I acknowledge mine aren't as unaltruistic and loving as yours, none the

less it is very important to me—considering that we have
its best interests at heart in other words, would it be so
hard to see whether we couldn't make a go of this
marriage?'

She considered for a long time then she said rather
bleakly, 'That's like asking a nation to love their in-
vaders. I don't think it's possible. I mean, for another
thing, there's the problem that you don't respect me—
you surely couldn't if you really believe that regular sex
is all I need to keep me happy——'

'There's a difference between regular sex and satisfying sex.'

She shot him an oblique look. 'Your ego is really
monumental, Justin, even for a man. All *right*, but I'm
still just another giddy girl to you, aren't I?'

'I suppose it wasn't a help possessing such stunning
looks on top of a father who spoilt you rotten, but you
certainly don't go out of your way to dispel that image,
Lucy.'

She looked across at him and there was something
curiously haughty in her eyes. 'Perhaps not, but that
might not be all there is to me. For example, I do know
quite a lot about Dalkeith and how it runs—if young
men can sow their wild oats, why can't girls have a few
giddy salad days, anyway?'

He put his knife and fork together and stared at them
for a long moment, before raising his eyes to hers. And
then there was something curiously enigmatic in them
as he said, 'I've told you, what's history can remain so.
Your legion of lovers and my—multitude of mistresses.
Unfortunately, you've got into the habit of sending out
unmistakable signals—you're probably right about

young Mr Lang and the kind of thoughts he's having about you now.'

Lucy grimaced.

'Not picking up the bait, Mrs Waite?' Justin said softly but with an undercurrent of mockery.

She tightened her mouth and subjected him to a deep blue look of considerable scorn.

He only laughed quietly. 'Just one more thing, Lucy. In case you haven't already got the message, if celibacy is becoming irksome then I am your only alternative. Remember that.'

She burst into speech. 'What about you? You don't really expect me to believe *I* am *your* only alternative.'

'Well, you are, so bear that in mind as well, my dear. But I'm afraid celibacy, inside marriage, certainly won't suit me forever.' He stood up. 'And you know, Lucy, while I give your devotion to Dalkeith full credit, there's no way a twenty-year-old girl could run it. There was no way you could have gone on without the kind of cash it needs again—and Dalkeith has become a rather expensive pastime for us Waites.' He stopped and watched her as she took the point and looked away uncertainly. Then he went on quite gently, 'But *this* way, here you are, mistress of it, and if you've got as much sense as I think you have in your more rational moments you must know it's in good hands. By the way, I'm taking a couple of weeks off and we're giving a house party this weekend. You might need to get in extra help. Goodnight.'

A couple of hours later, Lucy walked into her bedroom and closed the door.

As part of the austerity measures her father had been forced to introduce before his death, there was no live-in house help on Dalkeith. In fact Lucy had cut short her bachelor of arts degree to come home and look after her father six months ago and after her marriage, a curious marriage to say the least, she'd decided to keep it that way. It gave her something to do, and she'd discovered that, in lieu of her deep interest in Dalkeith being taken seriously, her interest despite herself in the crops Justin planned to grow and the sheep it still ran across its thousand acres of outback western New South Wales, that only left her horses for her to occupy herself with. And two mares in foal and two gelding hacks, devoted to them though she was, didn't take up a lot of time.

She did have a cleaning lady who came in daily and a farmhand to tend the fireplaces, but it had come as some surprise to her, in those last days of her father's decline, to find that she enjoyed cooking and gardening.

She sighed suddenly, pushed herself away from the door and picked up the silver-framed photo of her father from her dressing-table. No matter the things that she'd come to suspect even before his death, such as his being eminently suited to being a gentleman of leisure but *not* a gentleman farmer, and what she'd discovered about him after his death—that he'd tried to rescue Dalkeith from the brink again by gambling on horses, despite it all, she'd loved him and, only three months later, still missed him unbearably at times. If nothing else he'd certainly loved her unstintingly, and he'd taught her all the things he held dear to his heart, among them riding, shooting and fishing. He'd also taught her about art and music, he'd taken her to faraway exotic places, he'd helped her to fix her taste in clothes and all manner of things and yes, spoilt her wildly. But he'd never foisted a stepmother on her after her own mother, whom she couldn't remember, had died. In fact, she suspected he'd never got over her mother's death, and certain things in life hadn't had much meaning for him after it. Including Dalkeith.

He'd also sent her to a very expensive convent school where the Mother Superior had been strong-minded enough to persevere with the motherless, precocious, mischievous and often downright naughty Lucy Wainright despite the battles royal they'd had since Lucy had been placed in her care at nine and a half, and she'd continued there until she was seventeen and a half. They'd even parted on terms of mutual respect and by that time quite some mutual affection, although each was loath to admit it.

But had her father, Lucy wondered, as she stared down at his handsome likeness, never really realised how much Dalkeith, above all else, had meant to *her*? That even in her giddy salad days when she'd been queening it over all and sundry—her eyes flashed briefly—it, even more than her father, had been the rock to come back to. Did she have more of her Scottish great-grandparents in her than he'd ever had? A spiritual affinity with the land that was like a physical tie? Had he not known that, without him and without Dalkeith, brave, bright Lucinda Wainright, darling of society, was in fact lonely and more than a little frightened? But he had known how much she loved Dalkeith; wasn't that why he'd never told her he'd lost half of it to Justin's father?

She pushed off her shoes and curled up in the pink velvet armchair beside the fireplace, and stared into the flickering flames with a faraway look in her eyes.

It was ironic but true that she had hero-worshipped Justin Waite as a child. It was also true that Justin had, without her quite understanding it, achieved the status of a hallmark in her mind during her adolescent years. A hallmark that she had involuntarily found herself measuring other boys, then men up against, and finding most of them wanting. This had also led her, once she'd left school and on the few social occasions that they had met, to treat him with cool hauteur, yet to experience an undoubted desire to be *noticed*.

'And he noticed,' she murmured a little bitterly, her cheeks feeling warm again. 'Although the only sign he ever gave of it was that hateful little glint of amusement in his eyes—I really do hate him now!'

She sat up breathing quickly but also feeling a curious mixture of confusion and guilt. Why hadn't she pressed her father for details about his rift with the Waites, despite his extreme reluctance to say more on the subject? Well, I did try, she admitted. And of course I know now that he couldn't bring himself to tell me what was going on—the fact that Riverbend did diversify and go into breeding racehorses with spectacular success must have been an awful blow to his pride, but why couldn't I have realised it at the time? And then what he did say, about us no longer being good enough for the Waites, set my back right up. With the result, she conceded gloomily, sinking back in the chair, that I made myself ridiculous by treating Justin the way I did. But did I really offend him enough for him to take this kind of revenge? To make me marry him although he didn't love me and so he can get all of Dalkeith? she asked herself miserably.

And answered herself a little tartly—apart from amusing him, I doubt it. I mean, I never *saw* him without some beautiful woman on his arm or doing something spectacular like playing polo or crewing on some twelve-metre yacht, and of course he then proceeded to make his own fortune.

She brooded darkly for a moment on how Justin had taken a run-down saddlery business and built it into a nationwide success story—another one—and so not only did Riverbend Stud produce top-flight progeny, but Riverbend Saddlery produced saddles of the finest quality, with an international reputation and all sorts of horse products, as well as clothing—riding boots et cetera. Yes, Justin was clever and not only with horses—and there was a ten-year age gap between them, damn it!

She got up and paced about angrily. 'So what?' she murmured to herself, and picked up her silver-backed hairbrush and turned it over and over in her hands. Then she stopped and looked down at it and fingered the ornate 'W' engraved into the handle, and drew herself upright and stared at her reflection with cold eyes. 'Just remember what he said when he proposed. He said, "We won't even have to change the monograms, will we? Surely that demonstrates what a *practical* arrangement it would be."'

But she shivered suddenly because, in a moment of rage and panic, she *had* accepted. And then, in a moment of further panic on her wedding-night had made her 'dramatic declaration'. That she'd never willingly sleep with him. Had she in fact been seriously unbalanced by grief and everything else?

CHAPTER TWO

'I NEED you. Justin——'

'Well, well——' Justin Waite put out a lazy hand and grasped his wife's wrist '—did my little lecture set you thinking, dear Lucy?'

Lucy closed her eyes, attempted to free herself to no avail and ground her teeth. 'I need to *talk* to you. About this party.'

It was a bright, chilly morning but Justin had apparently been up well ahead of her, which was how she'd encountered him coming in through the kitchen door as she was on the way out. Normally she'd have kept on going.

'Ah.' He released her wrist. 'Then talk away while I start my breakfast.'

'What have you been doing?' she said involuntarily as she followed him reluctantly back into the kitchen where his breakfast was keeping warm on the range. He had on jeans, boots and a yellow sweater, his thick dark hair was ruffled and the cold morning air seemed to have agreed with him. In other words he looked fit, tough and capable, alert and slightly mocking, and more than a match for her. But when did he look any different these days? she wondered bitterly.

'I've been out and about,' he said idly, and carried the plate of sausages, scrambled eggs and toast to the kitchen table. There was a pot of coffee bubbling gently on the stove.

Lucy went over to it and poured two mugs which she carried to the kitchen table and sat down opposite him. 'You can tell me, you know. Not only is the place still half mine but I'm *interested*,' she said with extreme frustration before she could stop herself. 'Wouldn't I under normal circumstances have some sort of voting power or some *say* in what you do?'

'I've only been inspecting fences in the twelve-mile paddock, Lucy,' he said mildly. 'I made no momentous decisions other than that they need repairing.'

Lucy drew a breath and thought how much she'd have enjoyed a gallop down to the twelve-mile before breakfast instead of the lonely, aimless ride she'd been about to take. 'What about the boundary rider's hut?' she asked tonelessly. 'The last time I saw it it was a bit ramshackle. Grandad always liked to keep it provisioned and weatherproof because the twelve-mile can flood, but it's on the only high ground, so if you did get marooned out there——'

'That too. They're starting on it today.'

She lowered her lashes instead of glaring at him. 'Well,' she said even more tonelessly, 'tell me about the house party. You haven't given me much notice.'

Justin spread marmalade on his toast. 'I can get someone in to do it all if you like. I have mentioned that there's no need for you to do so much of your own work, Lucy.' He put the lid on the marmalade with some impatience.

'And I've told you, I'd go round the bend that way, Justin, not to mention feeling as if I was on the receiving end of your patronage.'

He smiled. 'I can assure you it's not patronage to provide one's wife with household help.'

'But then we've agreed I'm not much of a wife. Look, I can do it. I can get Mrs Milton and her sister to come up—as I've done before on Dalkeith.'

'Then do it,' he said curtly. 'What do you want to know?'

'When they're arriving, when they're leaving, who they are and just what kind of a weekend you have in mind!'

'Why, the kind of weekend Dalkeith is famous for, Lucy,' he said blandly. 'I'm sure I don't have to tell you. There'll be four guests and Sasha.'

She stared at him then forced herself to relax. 'Well, if they come on Friday afternoon, we'll have an informal dinner, a buffet and a simple evening—music, cards and so on. Saturday, a picnic at the creek, some sightseeing around the place, some target shooting or archery, a little gentle croquet for the ladies, then a formal dinner to which I could invite some locals.' She considered. 'Yes, I could invite the Simpsons, and Miles Graham for Sasha! That should even things up.' Her eyes glinted. 'Then on Sunday morning a late breakfast, and they can do what they like until they leave after lunch.'

'And you and Mrs Milton and her sister can cope with all that?' he queried.

Lucy shrugged. 'They've got it down to a fine art. Mrs Milton does the cooking, although a lot of it is prepared beforehand, and her sister makes the beds, tidies up, waits on table et cetera. It's all in the preparation, Justin. So long as you feed people really well, the rest seems to take care of itself.'

'It's Tuesday today, Lucy,' he warned.

'That gives me three full days, Justin,' she said wearily. 'Besides, I think I need a challenge,' she murmured, and propped her chin on her hands.

He regarded her steadily then said quietly, 'You're making things awfully hard for yourself, Lucy.'

'No, you're making them hard for me, Justin.'

'I hesitate to labour this point, but if it weren't for me you wouldn't be here.'

'Perhaps. But I might have felt I'd gone down in a fair fight—who knows?'

'How are you going to handle us in front of these people?'

She blinked, then grinned. 'I hadn't thought of that—yet.' She sat up suddenly and tossed the thick plait she'd braided her hair into over her shoulder. 'Do you mean we'll have to put on a loving show?'

'It's not unexpected in newly-weds,' he observed.

'Oh.'

'And I don't expect I'd take kindly to being made a fool of,' he added without the least emphasis, yet a curious underlay to his words that made her nerves prickle oddly. Perhaps it was something in his eyes as well, as they rested on her.

She opened her mouth, closed it then said with dignity, 'It's not a pre-requisite to... I mean, some of the people I've known who really were in love didn't...sort of flaunt it.'

'Perhaps not,' he agreed. 'What I'm trying to get at is, are you prepared to be sensible or are you going to cook up something like yesterday to advertise to the world that we're not in love?'

Lucy pursed her lips. 'I might just be normal and let them work it out for themselves,' she said thoughtfully.

'I don't think you can expect much more from me, Justin.'

'When you say normal, do you mean you'll include me in your *come hither*——?'

'I *don't* do that,' she cut in sharply.

'Perhaps you don't realise you're doing it. Perhaps it's second nature now. Didn't you notice Robert Lang going weak at the knees when you smiled at him yesterday?' He lifted a dark eyebrow at her.

Lucy set her teeth.

He waited then gathered his plate and took it over to the sink.

'I can't help how I smile!' she said in a goaded sort of voice at last.

'No, but with a bit of age and maturity you should be able to use it with discretion. Otherwise you could find yourself in a situation you might find hard to handle one day.'

Lucy tossed her head and stood up, with not the slightest idea, as he came back to the table, what he had in mind. 'Like this,' he said softly, standing right in front of her so she had to tilt her head back, and taking her in his arms as her eyes widened. 'In the position of being kissed by your sworn enemy.'

Her lips parted. 'Justin...'

But he ignored both the look in her eyes and the incredulity in her voice, and held her closer so she couldn't help being aware not only of the feel of his hard, muscled body against her own but of the faint tang of aftershave and sheer maleness about him—and finding it curiously heady, like some primitive assault on her senses. This both stunned her slightly and made her less able to cope with what followed. A searching, not particularly deep kiss to which she didn't respond particularly yet which didn't exactly repel. It was really strange, she reflected afterwards. It was as if her body had gone languid and her mind was suspended above her, recording and storing the event, monitoring her own reactions but, above all, searching for his.

And when he lifted his head at last she blinked once then stared into his eyes, with her heart in her mouth suddenly at what she might see.

What she did see was the way he narrowed his eyes immediately, and then the little laughter-lines beside them creased. 'Well, Lucy,' he said wryly, 'you have got that down to a fine art, haven't you?'

She licked her lips and said huskily, 'What do you mean?'

His hands slid down her back to her waist and he lifted her off her feet and moved her away, and steadied her but didn't take his hands away. 'The art of kissing and giving nothing away at the same time.'

A tinge of pink came to her cheeks and a pulse beat at the base of her throat, a pulse of anger as it happened. 'If that's not exactly what you did, I'll eat my hat,' she retorted, and removed herself from his grasp but sat down almost immediately.

'Then why are you so cross?' He leant against the corner of the table and folded his arms.

'Perhaps I'm tired of having it continually pointed out to me what a *femme fatale* I am.' She picked up the lid of the sugar bowl and replaced it not gently. 'And if that was a warning of the deluded sort you were issuing yesterday——'

'It was a warning to behave yourself this weekend, Lucy.'

'*Listen*, Justin!' Her eyes were a deeper, decidedly stormy blue now.

'No, you listen to me, Lucy.' He unfolded his arms and pinned one of her wrists to the table as her hand wandered towards the sugar bowl again, and he lifted her chin in his other one, also not gently as she resisted stubbornly. And his eyes were a cold, hard grey as he said, 'You can fight me all you like in private, but not in public, because if you do, I'll retaliate, believe me, in a way you wouldn't like at all, and in a way that will make your little war look like child's play. Do we understand each other?'

It was Mrs Milton who broke into Lucy's reverie. Mrs Milton came in daily and Lucy was still sitting at the kitchen table where Justin had left her, staring into space, as she arrived.

'Morning, Miss Lucy,' she said brightly and placed a parcel on the table. 'There's those sheets that needed mending.'

'Oh!' Lucy jumped. 'Oh, thank you, Mrs Milton— sorry, I was miles away. How are you?'

'Fine, love. Miles away where?' Mrs Milton poured herself a cup of coffee.

Lucy grimaced. 'Are you doing anything this weekend? You and your sister?'

'No. Got a party on?'

'Yes, and I want it to be—something special, Mrs Milton. Hang on, I'll get a pen and paper.'

Whether by design or not, Justin stayed out of her way over those next three busy days, although they did meet for breakfast on the Wednesday morning.

'You have a dirty mark on your chin, Lucy,' her husband said after a more formal greeting had got him a cool look and a barely audible murmur in reply.

This time she responded with a raised eyebrow and a shrug, causing him to narrow his eyes and appear to drop the subject. But as they passed each other later, he stopped her with a hand on her shoulder and put his forefinger on the 'mark' on her chin.

'Did I do that?'

She merely nodded.

He took his finger away and inspected the faint blue bruise. He also let his gaze wander over her mouth, innocent of any lipstick yet rose-pink and finely chiselled, the smooth lucent skin of her cheeks, the deep pansy blue of her eyes with their sweeping lashes, darker than her hair, and the escaping tendrils of wheat gold curling on her forehead. 'My apologies,' he said. 'I didn't know you bruised so easily.'

'I don't bruise so easily. Perhaps you don't know your own strength. Or perhaps you do.'

'What I haven't known,' he said with a twist of his lips, 'is anyone quite as stubborn as you. I suppose you've now added the fact that I'm a callous brute to your list of my sins.'

'Some of your threats left me in no doubt of it at all even before this,' she murmured coldly. 'May I go now? I have a lot to do.'

'How's it going?'

'It's all under control.'

'Do you need any assistance? From me,' he said gravely.

Her look spoke volumes. 'All you have to do is be here, Justin.'

'I still haven't told you who's coming—apart from Sasha.'

Lucy shrugged. 'I rang Sasha myself and got it all from her. She was a mine of information, in fact. Two couples, although one unmarried couple who will nevertheless share a bedroom——'

'Unlike some *married* couples I know. I wonder if it's a new trend? Go on,' he said politely.

'Yes, well,' Lucy said evenly, 'Sasha also told me that although it's not strictly a business weekend, they will be inspecting some yearlings at Riverbend on their way here and might be interested in buying them at the upcoming yearling sales in Sydney—she said that very significantly, Justin. In other words—don't rock the boat, Lucy, *if* you can help it! And, she also gave me some helpful suggestions which——'

'You will go out of your way to ignore,' Justin said amusedly.

'Indeed I will.' Lucy's eyes flashed briefly, recalling Sasha's helpful advice which had included the maxim that keeping things simple might be a good idea. 'How you put up with her I've no idea!'

'I've told you, she's very good at her job.'

'She's certainly got a superiority complex. Is that why you two get along so well?' she asked innocently, and went on impatiently, 'Besides, being good at your job doesn't mean you have to be treated as a friend, necessarily.'

'Well Sasha is both actually, Lucy. And since I moved to Dalkeith, so that you might remain in your ancestral home,' he said and held her eyes in a suddenly cool look, 'she is more up to date on matters relating to the stud and this crop of yearlings than I am. So she will be here

in what you might call an unofficial business capacity.'
He paused then added with that same cool look. 'Don't
upset Sasha, Lucy. She may rub you up the wrong way
but she has a brain like a computer when it comes to
horses, and extremely good judgement.'

'As a matter of fact I believe you, Justin. I've even
thought she has a certain horsey look about her—nothing
less than a chestnut thoroughbred with wonderful lines,
of course!' she finished with a grin. 'As for upsetting
her,' she added, 'I wish you would tell me how to, because it doesn't seem possible.'

They stared at each other—rather, Lucy found it suddenly impossible to evade his gaze or to understand why
it made her suddenly feel a bit small, but it did and she
said at last, 'Oh, all right! I *won't* upset Sasha—so far
as it's humanly possible for me not to!'

'Good.' He said nothing more but moved out of her
way.

'Am I being dismissed now?' she demanded.

'Why not?'

'There are times, Justin Waite, when you irritate the
life out of me,' she said precisely. 'And what with you
and Sasha telling me what I should do and what I
shouldn't do, it will be a miracle if this weekend doesn't
turn out to be a disaster——' She broke off and made
a disgusted sound.

'And there are times, Lucy, when it's impossible to
tell you anything—I wouldn't be too happy about this
weekend turning into a disaster, so if you have any doubts
tell me now.'

'*I* don't——'

'I suppose the proof of that will be in the pudding,'
he said drily, and studied her. 'By the way,' he said,

flicking his gaze over her denim overalls, and the two
pigtails she wore her hair in, 'Would you mind not
wearing your hair like that over the weekend?'

She blinked. 'Why not—as if I would, anyway.'

'I could be accused of cradle-snatching, that's all. Off
you go.'

'Perhaps you are!'

'Now, Lucy, we both know I'm not. Don't we?' His
grey gaze bored into hers until she reddened and turned
away abruptly and angrily but without words.

Fortunately for her seething state of mind, there was
enough to be done to calm her and force her to concen-
trate—and not only that. There was the knowledge that
both Justin and Sasha had doubts about her capabilities
as a hostess. In her less angry moments she recognised
that it was a useful spur, in her more angry moments
she told herself she would certainly show them a thing
or two. And by Friday midday the fruits of her labour
and Mrs Milton's were very evident. The house was polished and shining and filled with flowers. The guest bedrooms were impeccable, with not a wrinkle in their
bedspreads, and the cold room was filled with a se-
lection of pies and pastries, cold meats, quiches, fruits
and vegetables and three splendid, plump ducks hung
there, ready to be roasted for Saturday night's dinner.

It was also not long past midday when disaster struck,
in the form of a distraught phone call from Mrs Milton
who'd gone to pick up her sister to take up residence in
the staff quarters for the weekend.

'...Your mother? Oh, I'm so sorry, Mrs Milton,' Lucy
said into the phone and a moment later, 'Yes, of course
if it's that serious, I do understand. Um...you and your

sister must be worried sick and will want to be with her...
Look, if there's anything I can do, please——'

'You've got enough on your plate as it is, pet,' Mrs
Milton said down the line in tones quite unlike her normal
cheerful ones. 'I've been racking my *brains* and all I can
come up with is my niece, Shirley. How would it be if
I send her up, Miss Lucy? She's a good cook, that I can
guarantee, and doesn't mind what she turns her hand
to. There's only one problem and that's——'

'Oh, Mrs Milton, please do,' Lucy said into the phone.
'I'd be so grateful, and between us we've done most of
it, haven't we? What's the problem?'

'Well she'd have to bring her son, Adrian——'

'That's no problem!'

'Mmm, I haven't told you about Adrian, have I?
Look, just...if you're *firm* with him he's fine, but his
father ran off when he was two, so... And Shirley worships the ground he walks on.'

'Don't worry, I'll tie him up if...no, of course not,
Mrs Milton, I wouldn't dream of it, but I'm sure we'll
be able to cope with him between us. Now you just worry
about your mother and give her my love—I'll be thinking
of you all.'

She put the phone down and took several deep breaths,
then remembered she'd forgotten to ask how old Shirley's
Adrian was.

He was ten, with red hair, prominent blue eyes and buck
teeth. He walked with a swagger and didn't reply when
spoken to. His mother had faded blonde agitated-looking
hair but otherwise was clean, neat and presentable and
obviously anxious to do her very best.

'Well, Shirley,' Lucy said with a dazzling smile, half an hour before the guests were due to fly in, 'I guess the important thing is not to panic. Everything in the buffet is either cold or only needs heating up so tonight will be quite simple, and I'll nip in later to give you a hand.' And she took Shirley step by step through the evening's requirements. Then she showed them to their room and showed Adrian the television and even fetched some of her old books and games for him.

'He's not much of a reader,' his mother said with an apologetic smile, 'but it's lovely of you to bother, Miss Lucy. Now, Adrian, you will be a good boy, won't you?'

At five-thirty, the long, lovely veranda room played host to the glow of lamplight, the chink of glasses and some exuberant conversation. And despite the fact that part of her mind was elsewhere, Lucy was in the thick of it.

She wore slim scarlet trousers, matching flat shoes and a cream pullover with a wonderful red, green and cream scarf worn shawlwise. Her hair was loose and she was faintly pink from some of the extravagant compliments she'd received—most on the subject of new brides and early wedded bliss. Their guests were of course all older than she was, the two women in the same mould as Sasha, elegant late twenties or early thirties, experienced and articulate and both with careers of their own. But apart from that aspect of it, it was a milieu she was very familiar with and one her father had taught her to hold her own in some years ago. She'd been hostessing his parties since she was about eighteen, after all. And if she had fewer resources to hand than she'd ever had before, plus one Dennis the Menace on hand, she was damned if anyone was going to know it. Least of all

Justin, although she'd caught him looking at her once or twice with something oddly alert in his eyes. But he's not a mind-reader, she reassured herself, and there's no earthly reason for him to go into the kitchen tonight, anyway. The longer I can keep him in the dark and still cope, the better, she reasoned—somewhat obscurely, she realised briefly, but didn't have the time to elaborate.

All the same, at six-thirty, when she suggested to everyone that they might like to freshen up although not to worry about changing, she breathed a sigh of relief when they all took themselves to their bedrooms and she repaired to the kitchen as unobtrusively as she could. To find Shirley standing in the middle of the room looking wild-eyed and tearful.

'What's wrong?' she demanded.

'He's gone!'

'Who?'

'Adrian! He could be anywhere out there! He's not a country boy, Miss Lucy; we're just spending a holiday with Auntie Vera!'

'The little... um, calm down, Shirley. I'll find him. You just keep on with the buffet. We've got an hour.'

It took her half an hour to locate Adrian in the loft above the garage. And the mild lecture she gave him brought no visible reaction from him even when she told him he'd frightened the life out of his mother. 'Now just stay put,' she admonished as she marched him back to his room. 'Tomorrow you can go out and see the horses, I'll organise a ride on a tractor for you, whatever you like—and your dinner's coming in a moment.'

* * *

'Are you all right, Lucy?'

'Fine, Justin,' she said brightly, finding him alone in the lounge. He'd added a sage-green sweater to his informal gear and his hair was brushed and tidy, his grey eyes watchful. 'No one down yet?'

'No. Have you been running somewhere?'

She laughed. 'No. Why?'

'You look a little—harassed. Are Mrs Milton and her sister coping all right?'

'Everything's fine. If you could just have some confidence in me, it would be a big help.'

'Very well, Lucy. Ah, here are the first of our guests.'

The buffet went off smoothly and with plenty of compliments and afterwards for a while they played music and all chatted together, and then the men tended to group together at one end of the room, leaving the women at the other and Sasha looking for once in her life as if she didn't quite know which group to join.

Lucy seized the opportunity and murmured in her ear that she'd be grateful if she could deputise for her for a moment, while she checked that all was well behind the scenes. Sasha looked gratified, as much, probably, Lucy reflected, that 'behind the scenes' should need checking. But she did as she was asked.

Behind the scenes, there was another story. The dining-room was cleared, the kitchen was tidy and a tea tray was set out but there was no sign of Shirley. What she was doing in fact, was swabbing out the staff bathroom and passage leading to it because Adrian had allowed the bath to overflow. He'd got so wrapped up in the television programme he'd been watching, his mother explained, he'd forgotten.

Lucy closed her eyes and counted to ten. And, on opening them, noticed Adrian watching her interestedly. Why, he's testing me out, she thought, the little wretch.

'Isn't it time he was in bed?' she said as mildly as she could.

By the time she got back she was feeling decidedly limp—it had taken the two of them a good twenty minutes of vigorous mopping to dam the flood, her feet were damp inside her shoes and she had trickles of sweat running down her back, but no one appeared to notice and the party had come together again and was dancing to the CD player.

'Oh damn,' she muttered to herself.

But two hours later her ordeal was ended, or so she thought. The party broke up at last and everyone went up to bed appearing happy and contented with their stay on Dalkeith so far.

'Let's hope I can keep it that way,' she murmured to herself as she tidied up. She'd sent Shirley to bed, reasoning that it might keep Adrian out of more mischief as well as having her bright and fresh for the next day. But when it was all done she stood in the middle of the dining-room, thinking about the three other women in the house, excluding poor Shirley.

Thinking about them in a context that surprised her a little. In other words, how much more appropriate any one of them would be as a consort for Justin than she was. How, for example, *they* would react to being told that without regular, satisfying sex they could become— what had he said—fractious and troublesome?

Well, she mused, she couldn't imagine him saying something like that in the first place. To them. So how would communication on the subject take place with someone older and wiser? A more sophisticated play on words? A simple expression of need—with Sasha he'd probably only have to crook his finger, she thought somewhat maliciously, then sighed.

But a moment later she discovered herself feeling a sense of righteous indignation—talk about her *come hither* smiles! Had he not noticed that despite two of their female guests being partnered there had been throughout the evening a discreet summing up of Justin taking place, an awareness—yes, very subtle, but *there*. Of course it was always there with Sasha and he must be blind not to notice it. Why didn't he? But not only that, her thoughts ranged on, a subtle summing up of herself had been taking place all evening, in the direct context of her suitability for Justin.

She stood in the middle of the dining-room deep in thought, wondering if it was all part of the games people with a bit of age and maturity played, wondering if he played it himself, or wondering finally if he just had this devastating effect on women and had got so used to it that he didn't notice it any more!

'*Lucy.*'

'Oh!' She turned with a start to find the object of her deep, dark musings regarding her with some amusement. 'You—I didn't hear you,' she said lamely.

'I gathered that. You seemed to be a hundred miles away.'

'Not really,' she replied ruefully. 'Well, that's all done. I think I'll go to bed now—goodnight.'

'I'm coming up myself.' He strolled beside her to the foot of the staircase. 'It was a very successful evening, by the way.'

Lucy paused with her hand on the banister and tried to think of something to say but ended up unsuccessfully trying to smother a huge yawn. 'Sorry, I——'

'You're exhausted. Come,' he said, and without further ado he picked her up and started up the stairs.

After a moment of supreme surprise, she lay quiet and composed in his arms, her lashes fanning her cheeks, her only thought to wonder what was coming.

But all he did was to put her down on her bed and turn away to stoke up her fire. She lay quite still, watching him and feeling an odd little sense of loss, which translated upon a moment's thought to the realisation that she hadn't felt quite so lonely or strung up in his arms as she did lying alone on her bed the way she was... She bit back a husky exclamation and sat up, feeling unreasonably annoyed and stung to retaliation.

'It's a pity we couldn't have done that for the benefit of the gallery,' she said ironically. 'Justin, is it important to you the kind of impression I make on these people? I mean, are they going to judge you on me, sort of thing?'

He straightened and came over to the bed. 'Why?'

'Why what?'

'Why are you asking me that, Lucy?'

She stared up at him. 'Why shouldn't I? I'm curious, that's all.'

He looked faintly sceptical but said, 'I guess it's human nature to wonder what people see in each other and make some sort of judgement.'

'So,' she said slowly, 'were I to be judged—if they were to think for example, well, she's pretty enough and all that but mightn't she bore Justin to tears after a while?—how will that affect how they think about you?'

He frowned. 'Lucy, if I knew what was behind this I might——'

'You're the one who wanted me to make a good impression and not look as if I'd been snatched from my cradle,' she broke in tartly.

He smiled. 'Is that how you've been feeling tonight? A little out of your depth? I thought you were a bit wrought up about something.'

The accuracy and the inaccuracy of his words brought a faint blush to her cheeks and a further sense of maltreatment to her heart. 'You can't have it both ways, Justin. You did marry me, even if it was for all the wrong reasons, but they don't know that, so——'

'Lucy,' he interrupted gravely, 'let me set your mind at rest. *I* don't give a damn what people think about my private life; I never have. My concern about how you might behave this weekend was motivated by this—when you invite people to spend time with you, especially way out in the backblocks like this where they can't get up and go that easily if they want to, I think you're fairly obliged not to make them feel uncomfortable and as if they're in the midst of a domestic brawl. Don't you agree?'

She opened her mouth, closed it then said scathingly, 'Of course! That doesn't explain the cradle bit, though.'

'Well, as to that,' he said musingly, and picked up a strand of her hair, 'I wondered if it mightn't be part of your strategy, that's all.'

Lucy blinked at him. 'I don't understand.'

'Don't you? I thought since I'd made it plain that your *femme fatale* act—your words, not mine, but not inappropriate—was something I wouldn't approve of you might—change tack.'

Lucy closed her eyes. 'Funnily enough, it didn't occur to me at all,' she said bleakly.

'You wouldn't be losing your grip on this—war, would you, Lucy?' he queried, slipping her hair through his fingers then smoothing it back into place and standing back a step.

For the briefest moment Lucy wondered if she was. But she said, 'I'm rather tired, Justin, that's all.'

'Is it, Lucy?'

The way he said it, on a different note entirely made her open her eyes. 'What more could there be?'

'Unless you tell me, I don't know.' His eyes searched hers.

She looked away and found herself considering telling him that she didn't have Mrs Milton and her sister, only one flustered and anxious substitute—and Adrian, and that if the rest of the weekend went well it would be something of a miracle—he'd probably find out soon enough, anyway. But almost immediately she decided she couldn't stand his scorn, not tonight, so she said wearily, 'There's nothing,' and lay back exhaustedly.

'Perhaps you're trying too hard, Lucy.'

She stretched her throat and rubbed it. 'I really don't know what I have to do to *make* you approve of me, Justin.'

He moved so his face was in the shadows and she couldn't read his expression. 'Just the one thing you won't do.'

For the life of her she couldn't help it, couldn't stem the images that flooded her mind, of lying in his arms and being made love to, of not being lonely, at least.

Images of surrender in the most complete way a woman could to a man, but... 'But then I might not approve of myself. It's a real dilemma, isn't it?' she whispered, and sat up suddenly with her hands to her face as hot tears sprang to her eyes. 'Please, just go away, Justin. I can't cope with you and all this at the same time.'

He stared down at her shaking shoulders for a long moment, then he said evenly, 'All right, I'm going. But if there is a problem you don't have to——'

'There's nothing!' She raised her tear-streaked face abruptly. 'Other than that you've now managed to undermine my self-confidence.'

'Why, Lucy, I never thought to hear you say that. Goodnight, my dear. Don't do anything stupid, will you?'

She didn't, not then, but before the weekend was over she seriously interfered with Adrian's freedom and committed a social solecism of considerable proportions.

CHAPTER THREE

IT WAS Sasha, who else, who broke the news on Sunday morning.

She came into the veranda room where everyone was lounging around comfortably just prior to getting ready to leave, still commenting on the great dinner party last night and lovely day they'd had yesterday, and she said into a lull in the conversation, 'Justin, there's a child handcuffed to a fence outside. He says Lucy did it and that she threatened to shoot him.'

Everyone sat up with wide eyes and turned to Lucy.

'Oh,' she swallowed, 'that's Adrian. He's only been there for about ten minutes. I . . .' She stopped and blushed bright red.

Incredibly, it was Justin who came to her rescue. 'What's he done now?' he said resignedly, and added for everyone's benefit, 'Adrian is the son of our cook, Shirley—a great cook, I'm sure you'll all agree.'

Lucy stared at him open-mouthed but he murmured gently, 'Tell us, Lucy, otherwise people will think you're some sort of a monster.'

'He . . .' Lucy licked her lips. 'Yesterday *he* hand-cuffed *me* to the towel rail in the kitchen. Um—one of his uncles is a policeman and he gave him this set. Fortunately his mother came to the rescue—eventually . . . And today,' she said hastily, 'he actually picked the lock of the gun cupboard—I caught him at it but of course luckily we keep the ammunition in a safe and I *didn't*

43

threaten to shoot him... but in light of the fact that he laid waste every tomato plant in the vegetable garden yesterday, lit a fire in the chicken shed and downed all the washing on the line in the duck pond, I thought some of his own medicine might be good for him... You *knew*!' she said to Justin. 'All the time you knew.'

'Not all the time. Where are the keys? I'll... let him out on parole.'

But a combination of all sorts of factors worked powerfully in Lucy and she was deaf to discretion. 'How could you?' she accused. 'Of all the low-down things! To let me go *on* pretending...oh!' She ground her teeth. 'I hate you, Justin Waite, you're the most arrogant, self-opinionated man I've ever met and that's only some of the things I hate about you.'

The silence was electric but Justin laughed, as if he was really amused. 'Well, we nearly made it,' he said obliquely. 'Sorry, friends, but Lucy has had a traumatic weekend, haven't you, my love? I'm sure you only need to apologise, though. To them, not necessarily to me,' he added, and his eyes mocked her.

Lucy glanced round, flinched visibly as no one's eyes quite met hers, then became aware of an agitated murmuring she was coming to know well behind her. She dug into the pocket of her jeans and removed a set of keys. 'Here you are, Shirley,' she said swinging round. 'He hasn't been there long and if I were you I'd confiscate those handcuffs—they're more of a temptation than some people can bear. I am sorry,' she said contritely, swinging back. 'I've been short-staffed this weekend and I have an unfortunate temper, apparently. I do hope you'll all forgive me.'

* * *

She lay on her bed with her eyes closed but knew it was Justin when she heard the door open and close. She'd heard the plane take off about half an hour earlier but she'd made her farewells—she winced as she thought of it—from the house.

What caused her to open her eyes was the sagging of the other side of her double bed, and she saw before she closed them again that, not content with sitting, he'd stretched out with his hands behind his head. He also said, 'You're not sulking, are you, Lucy?'

She sat up abruptly and crossed her legs. 'No. I'm still angry as a matter of fact, so if you've come to *lecture* me you're wasting your time.'

'The thought never crossed my mind,' he murmured.

She frowned then turned to him. 'Aren't you—angry?'

'Do I look it?'

She hesitated because in fact he looked perfectly relaxed and at home and there was only a sort of bland query in his eyes. 'I—there are times when I don't understand you, Justin,' she said at last.

'That's rather obvious.'

'I mean, I've just done the one thing you didn't want me to do: discomfited our guests in other words—yet you——'

'They *were* on their way out, but go on.'

She breathed deeply. 'All right. I displayed sentiments not exactly common to new brides, I'm sure; I probably gave them cause to wonder whether I wasn't round the bend, handcuffing children to fences! Isn't that enough?'

'And all without even trying.' He smiled unexpectedly. 'Are you so annoyed because you feel its sheer spontaneity robbed it of malice aforethought and robbed you therefore of some satisfaction?'

Lucy bit her lip.

'As for my—low actions, what actually happened was that I knew something was up so I bearded a lady I *thought* must be Mrs Milton's sister in the kitchen yesterday morning, only to have the whole sad story explained to me—although she didn't tell me what a monster young Adrian is. I then acted as if I'd in fact known and decided to resume my mantle of ignorance with you mainly because you did seem to be coping admirably and I thought it would help restore your confidence. That same confidence you accused me of undermining. I now realise I should have bucked in and helped or something like that but then that would have meant explaining to people like Sasha——'

'That I'd got myself in a bind,' Lucy said gloomily.

'I thought you might not appreciate that.'

'I wouldn't have.' She pulled a fold of the bedspread through her fingers. 'Well,' she said grudgingly after some thought, 'I suppose I'm now in the wrong on all counts.'

'Is that an olive branch?' he queried.

She shrugged. 'Of a kind. Which means we're only back to square one, so——'

'Don't get any ideas, Justin. In other words.' He said it with utter gravity but when she looked at him there was a wicked little glint in his eyes.

She turned away hastily with her heartbeat doing an odd tattoo. 'I still have to live with the thought of at least five people seriously wondering about me,' she said with a toss of her head.

'I wouldn't worry about that; one of them even suggested you could be pregnant,' he said placidly.

'Well, I'm not!' Lucy sprang off the bed agitatedly.

'You know that and I know that, but they don't.' He stretched his arms lazily.

'In a few months' time they're all going to know it. What will they think then?' she demanded.

He regarded her in silence for a moment. 'Things could change in a few months' time.'

She made an exasperated sound and stalked over to the window. 'I still can't understand why you're quite happy for everyone either to know I do hate you or to think I have such a volatile disposition you must have been mad to marry me!'

'I told you, I don't give a damn what people think. I also happen to prefer you when you're being spontaneous, even if a shade volatile, Lucy.'

She stared out of the window. It had started out as another bright, cold day but it was pouring now. She shivered. 'Remind me to be spontaneous the next time... it happens.'

There was silence, then she tensed as she heard the bed springs creak, but she refused to turn even when she heard his soft footfall across the carpet stop right behind her. She said, with her tension reflected in her voice, 'Where do we go from here?'

'I don't know. Any ideas?'

She couldn't contain herself any longer. She swung round. '*No*. I'm the hostage, don't forget.'

'You're also seriously overtired and overwrought,' he said impatiently. 'Why don't you have a bath and go to bed?'

'At three in the afternoon!' she said jerkily. 'Apart from anything else, Adrian is still on the loose——'

'He's not. I've had a chat with Adrian and I doubt if we'll have any more trouble with him. I've also told

Shirley to relax for a couple of hours and thanked her for her considerable efforts.'

'And she's no doubt got stars in her eyes now and thinks you're just marvellous,' Lucy said bitterly.

He raised a mocking eyebrow. 'Being bitchy doesn't become you, Lucy.'

'I wish I knew what did—other than gracing your bed! As a matter of fact I also thanked Shirley and apologised for what I did to Adrian,' she said with irony.

'Then you won't mind if they stay on for a few days. Shirley to help you and Adrian to perhaps benefit from some male supervision.'

Lucy's eyes widened causing him to say with genuine irritation, 'He's only a kid suffering from the lack of a father. As a kid yourself who suffered from the lack of a mother, surely——'

'Oh, shut up, Justin,' she broke in. 'Don't you think I feel guilty enough as it is? In any other circumstances I'd never have...' She grimaced. 'I was just surprised you would want to take the time, that's all. Is that really——' she hesitated '—what you feel is the root cause of all my so-called problems, as a matter of interest? The lack of a mother?'

He shrugged. 'It mightn't have helped.'

'Thank you,' she said very formally, and added, 'Do you know what? I think I will do as you suggested after all. There just doesn't seem to be any alternative.'

'There is,' he said drily. 'And one day you'll take it, Lucy. Because I'll tell you what it is. Assuming you and I were in any kind of mental unity—let's leave the physical aspect out of it for the time being.' He smiled but it didn't reach his eyes. 'Assuming we were mentally attuned, we could go downstairs and have tea in front of the fire in the library, we could discuss the plans I have for the next week, all to do with Dalkeith and the kind of things that have been begging to be done for years, you could play the piano for a while—it's that kind of afternoon and I would enjoy listening while I read the papers the plane brought in this morning—then we could have dinner, watch a video and go to bed early. You would sleep like a top and be all bright-eyed and bushy-tailed in the morning.'

Her lips had parted as he spoke and she stared into his eyes with a kind of longing dawning in her own, which he saw, but he made no movement, no gesture.

She turned away.

She took a long bath and in a sudden spirit of urgency tried to sort out her thoughts in the process and to reduce her dilemma to stark facts rather than overheated, panicky emotion.

But the results *were* stark, she decided as she added more hot water and stared dismally through the steam. She was married to a man who didn't love her, who'd stood to gain by marrying her and had virtually forced her into it. A man, she mused, who must have taken a conscious decision that a marriage of convenience suited him best and had possibly decided he could mould her into the the kind of wife he wanted. What kind of man would do that? A man with a grudge, perhaps, yet it wasn't really *his* affair, more his father's, and it seemed an extreme length to go to surely, especially when he could have had virtually any wife he chose. No, there had to be more to it, she reflected, and wondered if there'd been anything in the Justin she'd known as a child to indicate this... hardness, sort of.

'He was always—I don't know,' she murmured to herself, 'you just knew he would always get what he wanted somehow, that's true. He was self-contained and...and of course, talking about mothers, he didn't have one either after she ran off with someone. Perhaps he suffered from a lack of it more than I did.' She sat up with a frown in her eyes. 'Perhaps that's why he thinks he can treat women like this: because he never had a woman he could respect or appreciate in his formative years. I bet that's got something to do with it!'

But a moment later she sank back ruefully, as it crossed her mind that coming from *her* this character-analysis of her worldly, sophisticated husband would probably be treated as laughable. Her thoughts ranged on. Assuming she did give in, she moved uncomfortably in the water then forced herself to consider the possibility. Assuming she did, what kind of a husband would he be for the rest of her life? Always a little distant, always the boss, so to speak—what kind of a marriage would that be? Or would she really, once she was *bedded*, be so besotted it wouldn't matter, or it would all come right in some mysterious manner she just couldn't foresee.

'And I *can't*,' she said with some force, 'because if he's an enigma now, he always will be, and even if he isn't a terrible husband it will only be half a life. Of course, there's always Dalkeith...is it such a price to pay?'

She shivered suddenly, and not because the water was cold but because it was occurring to her more and more that she was going to have to pay a price for her beloved home.

* * *

She also slept for a couple of hours, something that was unheard of for her during the day but although she woke feeling less tired she also felt cold and lonely as the rain-laden dusk blotted out the landscape. She pulled on a navy-blue tracksuit and sat brushing her hair for a long time, staring at her image in the mirror because it was in her mind to take a step she hadn't believed she ever would...

Justin was reading the papers in the library as she entered and closed the door behind her. He raised his dark head and watched her thoughtfully as she stood just inside the door, her hand still on the handle as if she might change her mind and leave again.

Then he said, 'Feeling better? Dinner's nearly ready, I believe.'

'Oh. Yes. I am. Justin——' She stopped as he stood up and was nearly overcome by nerves and by something else. A sudden sense of frustration, because knowing Justin Waite was like knowing the cover of a book you'd never read and because there were some ways she knew him that were infinitely disturbing, and not things she'd taken into account during her bathtime analysis of her situation. Things, for example, that only struck her when she was in his presence—or in his arms. Things like the feel of him and the feel of his mouth on hers, the easy strength of his arms and shoulders. And the knowledge that he was a dangerously attractive man, and suddenly being in the position of having to admit to herself that she'd always known it and that no amount of taboos on him could make her completely immune to it. It had been there, of course, when she'd been measuring other men up to him, there when she'd resolutely ignored him but noted every little detail of the women he was with.

There now, as he stood watching her looking big and casual in his jeans and green sweater—and the treacherous thought came to her that if she just walked across the room into his arms, if he would just hold her and perhaps smooth her hair and touch her face gently, before he did anything else, it *might* all come right...

'Justin.' She released the door-handle and took a couple more steps. 'What you said earlier,' she went on hurriedly, 'about being *mentally* attuned. Could we—talk about that a bit more?'

His lips twisted but he said after a moment, 'Sure. Would you like a pre-dinner drink to—help it along?'

'Thanks,' she murmured and sat down opposite his chair.

He poured her a brandy and soda and one for himself and came back but didn't sit. Instead he propped an elbow on the mantelpiece and sipped his drink, not looking at her. 'Go ahead.'

Lucy took a large swallow of hers. 'Would it compromise me if I said,' she paused and licked her lips, 'if I said I could give it a try?'

'Compromise you how?' he enquired.

'I mean, would it lead you to think that it's a preliminary to going to bed with you?' she said tartly.

He considered gravely. 'Probably.' He lifted his head at last and there was amusement in his grey eyes.

She tried consciously to stem the tide of pink that came to her cheeks but of course that wasn't something one could consciously control so she said evenly, 'Well, you'd be wrong.'

He moved his shoulders briefly and murmured, 'My mistake. What would it mean, Lucy?'

She hesitated then said honestly and bleakly, 'I can't think what else to do, that's all.'

'Are you proposing, in other words, that we spend the rest of our lives in only mental affinity?'

Her nostrils flared and she took a huge swallow of her brandy this time which caused her to cough and splutter a bit before she got out, 'I can't *think* that far ahead! All I'm suggesting is that—all I'm saying is that I can't go on like this. I'm...I just don't know what else to do. For the moment. And while I'm in this awful situation, which is all your fault, don't forget, life is sort of slipping away from me and I feel useless and...' She gestured helplessly.

He studied her in silence for quite some time and until her nerves started to prickle. Then he said, 'You're very young, aren't you, Lucy.'

'Are you asking me or telling me?'

He smiled faintly. 'Telling you, I guess. All right, we can give it a try. So long as you understand I won't be content with it forever.'

She raised her eyebrows ironically, 'Who knows, things might change in a few months.'

'Yes, well, you're also very articulate, my dear,' he said drily, 'for someone so curiously...naïve, sometimes.'

'That's a change—again. Has it occurred to you, Justin, that you haven't really worked out what I am?'

'On the contrary, I know exactly what you are, Lucy. I wouldn't be married to you if I didn't.'

Her eyes narrowed and another faint flush stained her cheeks and her heart started to pound uncomfortably. But he can't know, she thought. Everything he's ever said has gone along with... 'And what would that be?' she asked with a quiver in her voice.

'Oh——' he shrugged and stared into the fire for a moment '—a bit confused, a bit volatile at times——' he lifted his head and that wicked glint was back in his eyes '—stubborn but not without courage, bright as a tack, possessing a sense of style—quite a lot of admirable virtues, in fact.'

'Is that a fact?' Lucy tossed her head and grimaced. 'Then I was right—I think I mentioned it to you before. I'm trainable in your eyes, aren't I? You really feel you can mould me into a suitable wife, don't you? You must also feel I'm not too far gone down the path of *femme fatality* to be redeemed, and of course I'm also a Wainright of Dalkeith, let's not forget that. I'm just wondering what I'd get in return—assuming I ever allowed you to mould me into anything. In other words, Justin, say I had ideas about the kind of husband I'd like you to be—am I allowed to do that?'

'Why not?'

She blinked.

'What did you have in mind, Lucy?' he asked casually.

'I...' It was one thing to tell yourself in a bathtub exactly the kind of husband you'd want him to be, another to tell him to his face, she decided darkly, as the words were curiously difficult to formulate.

'I've always held the theory that honesty and openness between men and women is the best way, if that's what you mean,' he said seriously after waiting politely for a moment. 'But women, some women,' he amended, 'find it rather difficult—uh—they have a natural reticence on the subject. Are you naturally reticent about those things, Lucy?'

'What ... what things?'

'How you like to be made love to, for example, how you like to be touched and what turns you on—all things that are really at the core of a marriage wouldn't you agree?' he said softly, and added, 'I certainly think it can make or break a relationship so, yes, if you have any preferences I'd be quite happy to go along with them.'

It was a moment or so before Lucy realised that her facial muscles actually felt stiff with effort. The effort not to contort with anger. Her voice, she realised, sounded even stiffer, but there was nothing she could do about it. 'I didn't mean that. Do you ever think of anything else?'

'Frequently.' His eyes were amused again. 'In the context of a marriage it just seems to spring to mind, however.'

'But there must be more to it!' she burst out. 'There should be *love*, otherwise you grow tired of each other. There should be—there shouldn't be the kind of unequal feeling our marriage would have to have, and the gaping chasm of me knowing I'm being altered and made suitable for you—of just not understanding you, Justin, and why you've done this!'

'Or why you agreed to it,' he said significantly.

'Or why I...' She stopped and sighed.

'What if I told you I had no desire to make you feel unequal, Lucy?' he said into the silence.

'But you do.' She grimaced at the slightly forlorn note in her voice. 'And just the fact that this is a marriage of convenience for you will always make me feel unequal and I'll always feel I don't understand you.'

'Is there anything, apart from the way I married you, that you particularly dislike or distrust about me, Lucy?'

She'd turned her head to stare into the fire dispiritedly but she looked up with a frown because there was no amusement in his voice now. And she saw that his eyes were rather intent as they rested on her.

'I... well...' She stared at him helplessly. He waited as her lips worked again but all she could say finally and foolishly was, 'Why?'

'I mean, does the thought of going to bed with me fill you with disgust and make your skin crawl, and do you seriously believe that I don't have the best interests of your beloved Dalkeith at heart?'

She stared at him fixedly and discovered she was breathing rapidly as she wondered frantically how to answer him. She licked her lips. 'I haven't *really* thought of going to bed with you; I——'

'Haven't you, Lucy?' His impenetrable grey gaze was nevertheless mercilessly compelling and her cheeks flamed right on cue.

She took a deep breath. 'Not... seriously, then.'

'What was the verdict—unseriously?' His lips twisted.

'I thought I mightn't feel so lo...' She stopped abruptly.

'So lonely?' he said very quietly.

'Yes,' she whispered.

'You wouldn't.'

'Justin,' she got up agitatedly, 'this——'

'What else did you think?' he overrode her. 'Any revulsion, Lucy?'

She closed her eyes. 'No. But that's not the same thing as *wanting* to, with every fibre of your being!'

'I agree, but it's a start. How many times have you really wanted to with every fibre of your being, Lucy?'

She tightened her lips. 'That's for me to know and you to worry about, if it worries you at all.'

'All right—what about Dalkeith?'

What about Dalkeith—the words seemed to reverberate through her brain. 'Yes,' she said and the word was torn from her, 'I think you do have its best interests at heart, but——'

'Then, Lucy, I think it's time you grew up and accepted that life isn't all roses and sweet dreams, and that, when reality comes, most of us pick ourselves up and make the best of it. And the reality is, I am—and I apologise for it, but I am—to some extent a disillusioned cynic, I do want Dalkeith, for a variety of reasons, and if you want it too, and as badly as you say, then this is the price tag for it. On the other hand, I wouldn't have married you if I hadn't believed that, while it might not have been made in heaven, it could be made to work. Many, many marriages have worked on less. Nor do I expect you to be grateful or feel patronised; in fact if you made it a *commitment* I wouldn't expect a passive, unequal-feeling wife at all. I'd expect and be happy to accommodate your feelings for this place as well as your spirit and your courage—and even those times you feel justified in losing your temper with me.' He stopped and lifted his head. 'Dinner's ready, by the way. I hear the bell. Bring your drink, it's quite informal tonight.'

It was, in fact, macaroni cheese served at the kitchen table in company with Shirley and Adrian.

Lucy managed to contain her surprise—she was still a bit dazed by what Justin had said anyway—and then there was this facet to him that she'd not suspected. That he'd take seriously the plight of one fatherless boy and his mother.

It was obvious he'd already worked a small miracle with Adrian. Not that Adrian was suddenly a model of virtue but his surliness had disappeared and he caused Lucy to all but choke when he handed her his handcuffs and said, 'Mum reckons you better keep these until I'm reformed.' And she recognised that, coming from Adrian, this was equivalent to an apology.

But there were more surprises in store. Justin remarked, 'It's school holidays, Lucy. Adrian has three weeks so he's going to stay with us——'

'And Mum too,' Adrian said through a mouthful of macaroni.

'Of course, darling,' Shirley said. 'Mr Waite's asked me to help you out for the three weeks, Miss Lucy, and he's going to set Adrian some chores every morning to make up for the...damage he did.' She blushed, then brightened. 'And if he's good, he's going to take him up in the plane and teach him to ride a horse and drive a tractor. Is that all right with you?' she added anxiously.

'Fine!' Lucy said heartily. 'Yes, that'll be great, Shirley.' But she avoided Justin's eyes because of two simultaneous thoughts she had—a sudden ridiculous affinity she felt with Adrian, and the rather indignant thought that, given the right time and circumstances, she could have managed him just as well. Why the affinity? she pondered. Oh, I get it. There are times when Justin makes me feel just like a recalcitrant child and times when he uses the reward system, the old donkey-and-carrot trick, she thought bitterly, just as he's doing to Adrian. And, just like Adrian, I've got the feeling I've met my match, she reflected.

She couldn't help brooding on this, but no one seemed to notice her reticence—she winced at the thought—as

Shirley responded to Justin's conversation yet didn't for a moment lose her deferential air, as if to assure him she would never take advantage of this lapse in normal household relations, and Adrian ate his way solidly through three helpings.

But as Shirley was bustling about, making coffee and clearing away, Lucy looked directly at her husband at last and said suddenly, 'Do I have to make a decision right now?'

'You could think it over for a few days.'

'I will.'

He smiled faintly and changed the subject—or did he? 'I thought of doing an aerial inspection tomorrow if it's stopped raining. Care to come?'

CHAPTER FOUR

The next week proved to be a comfortable, peaceful one—for the most part.

They did all the things Shirley had enumerated and Adrian trod the road of being "reformed" quite successfully while Lucy discovered herself delighted to be included in the goings on of the property for a change—for the most part. It did sometimes sadden her to realise how neglected it had been, and occasionally it irked her to watch Justin in the role of owner, a role he played not flamboyantly at all but with a cool, businesslike practicality, a deep knowledge of the needs of Dalkeith and the unmistakable aura of a man who was not to be trifled with.

Like the great white hunter, she thought irreverantly once, but was conscious that she couldn't help secretly admiring his stewardship of her home at the same time. Which places me in an awkward position and no doubt induces this ambivalence in me, she thought with some bitterness.

It was that same afternoon that she was in her bedroom trying to decide what to wear to a dinner party being given by their nearest neighbours, twenty-five miles away, that Justin walked in on her as she was conducting a conversation with herself.

'Why, Lucy,' he murmured, stopping on the threshold and raising an eyebrow at the colourful array of clothing that littered the bed, 'are you moving out? And I thought I heard voices.'

Lucy put her hand on her hip and surveyed him imperiously. 'I was talking to myself, something I do frequently and always have—perhaps you should take that into account if you intend to persist in being married to me. And I'm trying to decide what to wear tonight—perhaps you should *also* take into account that it can sometimes take me *days*, let alone hours, to decide what to wear.'

'Dear me,' he said gravely. 'Mind you, that's not uncommon in women.'

'It may not be,' she replied with a toss of her head, 'but I don't intend to change.'

'I'm not asking you to. On the other hand——' he strolled over to the bed and picked up a dress '—husbands can be quite useful at times likes these.' He picked up a dress. 'I don't believe I've seen you in this one.'

It was a grey flannel straight dress with long sleeves and a white, lace-trimmed collar and cuffs. 'Funnily enough,' Lucy said. 'I'd almost——' She stopped abruptly.

'Almost decided on it?' he said with a lazy lift of an eyebrow. 'I'm quite sure you're about to change your mind, then.'

Lucy bit her lip and said stiffly, 'I'm not that stupid.'

'Why don't you give me a preview, then?'

'Why should I?'

'We could both reassure ourselves it's the right dress for the occasion. This is the first time we've been invited out as a couple,' he added.

'I know that only too well,' Lucy said with irony.

'Is that why you're a bit worked up?' he queried. 'You shouldn't be. We've both known the Gardiners for as long as we can remember.'

'Who said I was worked up?' Lucy countered coolly, because she would rather die than admit she *was*, on top of everything else, at the prospect of having to parade with Justin before a set of people she had known all her life, but as Lucy Waite now. 'Anyway, if I am it's not without cause,' she added shortly. 'I feel——' she paused '—I feel like a yearling about to go on display.'

Justin moved away from the bed and sat down in her pink velvet armchair. 'Sometimes you remind me of a long-legged yearling,' he commented. 'Why don't you try this dress on so I can give you the benefit of my wisdom on the subject?'

'Not with you sitting there—I mean...'

He scanned her jeans and jumper. 'I presume you have underwear on?'

'Of course I do, but I'm not about to even give you a glimpse of my underwear,' she said virtuously.

'Is it—particularly saucy?' he suggested with a perfectly straight face.

'It's not saucy at all; well——' Lucy hesitated '—all underwear is——'

'Suggestive?' He laid his head back and his eyes were wickedly amused although his face was still straight.

Lucy frowned. 'Justin—this conversation doesn't become you, you know,' she said scathingly then. 'In fact I find it particularly gratuitous, if you must know!'

'I don't think it is, not between a husband and wife, Lucy,' he replied politely, and stayed where he was, apparently perfectly relaxed in her favourite chair. 'But if you'd care to change in your bathroom, I wouldn't mind.'

Lucy muttered something beneath her breath then scooped up the dress and went to do just that. But once out of her jeans and jumper she looked at herself in her pretty white underwear with little red bows and felt a *frisson* run down her spine as she wondered several things. How would she look to a worldly, experienced Justin Waite in said underwear, and why was he doing this? But the most concerning of her mental processes was the undeniable little mesh she suddenly found herself caught in of being so aware of him sitting only feet away and then, like a tide growing in her and causing her to tremble foolishly, the thought that she could go out to him as she was, the thought *again* that she could stop fighting and put it all into his hands; this was a perfect opportunity to do just that...

Is that what he's trying to create? she asked herself, and observed that her eyes were wide and stunned in the mirror. The next instant she was climbing into the grey flannel dress hastily.

'There!' She glided out of the bathroom, did a couple of pirouettes and came to rest in front of the pink chair. 'I do think we're right about this dress, Justin. I'm quite sure the Gardiners would approve, anyway; they're extremely strait-laced and absolute sticklers for modesty and propriety, aren't they, fond as I am of them? And I wouldn't be at all surprised if Colonel Howard is there, and he's a real old fuddy-duddy, fond as I am of *him*, so—I will wear it.'

For a couple of moments Justin simply stared at her and Lucy was quite sure, with a piercing sense of embarrassment, that he knew exactly why she was talking nineteen to the dozen, and knew the rest of her tangled emotions all too well also. And she held her breath as their gazes locked.

But at last he stood up, although he still said nothing as he smoothed the lace-trimmed collar about her throat and let his gaze linger down the lines of her figure beneath the grey flannel that ended just above her knees. Then he said gently, 'Yes, dear Lucy, it is a model of modesty and propriety. You look almost Quakerish in it. However, you also look young and lovely and infinitely desirable, as I'm sure even Colonel Howard and the Gardiners will recognise.'

Her eyes widened and she could feel his hand that still rested on her shoulder as if it was burning through the cloth, as well as being devastatingly aware of everything else about him that attracted her so much, she thought with a jolt. The tall, lean lines of his body, the clever eyes... So much...she thought with another jolt, and said because she couldn't help herself, 'Do you mean that in a general way? Of course you do, how silly of me.' She swallowed and went on hurriedly, 'Well, I can't think of what else to wear, I mean that would be less——'

'Lucy.' He put a finger to her lips. 'The dress is fine, in fact it's perfect for you, but then so would sackcloth be, probably.' He smiled slightly, but not with his eyes. 'And yes, I did mean in a general way—but also in a very private way, and by that I mean just between the two of us. When you're ready to acknowledge and accept that, my dear, I promise you life will be a lot easier.' He stepped away and said then, perfectly normally and with a slight grimace, 'I guess it's time I got changed.'

* * *

'Well, it wasn't such an ordeal after all, was it?'

'No,' Lucy said quietly as they drove through the dark, chilly night back to Dalkeith.

'You're very quiet,' Justin said a couple of miles further on.

'Sorry.'

'Lucy, you've got me seriously worried,' he said wryly.

She moved restlessly and wondered how he would react if she told him he'd got *her* seriously worried. 'It's nothing, I'm just tired,' she said, and managed to yawn right on cue because she was a bit tired as well as everything else. 'It's quite a tiring business playing at being a wife, you know, Justin,' she added, and could immediately have kicked herself.

But he didn't make the rejoinder she expected. He drove on in silence, although he did speed up rather abruptly while she held her breath then cast a curious glance at him from beneath her lashes. But all she could see was the familiar angle of his jaw, the way his hair lay, thick and dark, and not much else as the powerful Land Rover chewed up the miles of the uneven, unmade road.

And some little devil of perversity was just about to prompt her into further, no doubt foolish observations, when there was a sudden dark shadow on the road in front of them, the Land Rover swerved wildly then skidded off the track, hit a large boulder with a sickening thump, came to rest at an angle with the engine cutting out—and Justin slumped forward over the steering-wheel.

'Oh, no! Justin! Are you all right. Oh, no!' Lucy scrambled on to her knees awkwardly on the seat and felt for a pulse in his neck. It was an all too familiar scenario on outback roads, either a kangaroo or some form of stray livestock bounding in front of a vehicle at the last moment, and then an unhandily placed boulder causing Justin to crack his forehead on the steering-wheel and knock himself out.

'That's all it is, please God,' she said to herself as she found a pulse, 'something temporary—oh, don't let him have fractured his skull or anything like that. And what do I do in the meantime?'

But after a few panicky moments she calmed down and decided all she could do was make him as comfortable as possible so, with quite some effort, she eased him back so his head was resting on the back rest. There was already a livid bruise on his temple, she saw by the interior light, and decided to apply a cold compress from the water bottle that no self-respecting vehicle travelled without, attached to its front bumper, in the bush.

So she climbed out, retrieved the thankfully undamaged water bottle, tried quickly to estimate whether the Land Rover would go again, and climbed back in because it was very cold.

It took him half an hour to come round.

Thirty minutes while the chill inside the vehicle grew, and it resisted all attempts to start the motor so she could have the heater on, and she stopped putting the compress on and concentrated simply on keeping them warm. Thirty minutes that felt like hours and acted in a strange and powerful way upon her for two reasons—the lurking, terrible fear in her heart that he might be more seriously injured but at the same time, the unaccustomed freedom of being able to look her fill upon him and not to have to hide anything from him...

Oh, dear, she thought, as she realised all this, it's no good trying to pretend I haven't fallen deeply in love with him, is it? It doesn't even help in the slightest to remind myself of all the injustices of the situation, not now when I'm alone with him like this, holding him and wanting to be nowhere on earth but here because he intrigues me and fascinates me and attracts me and I fear for him—and I can't imagine life without him.

Indeed, she was still looking her fill with her head on his shoulder, her arms around him, when his eyes fluttered open, and although they were dazed with pain, his lips twisted into a semblance of a smile as he said, 'Lucy? Is it you?'

Her heart lurched and her breasts felt curiously heavy and her stomach tightened beneath a sudden onslaught of sheer longing for him that told its own tale. 'Yes, it's me,' she said softly, sitting up. 'I'm trying to keep you warm—you hit your head. How do you feel?'

He groaned and gathered her back against him. 'Like hell.'

'Justin,' she said urgently.

But he chuckled huskily and stilled her movement. 'No, I'll survive. I just didn't feel like letting you go.'

Lucy subsided but only briefly. 'Are you sure you haven't fractured your skull or something,' she said anxiously, but didn't move as he started to stroke her hair.

'Quite sure—well, reasonably sure. It's all coming back now. Did I do much damage to the Land Rover?'

'It won't start. We hit a big rock——'

'Are you all right, Lucy?' He pushed her away a little at last and looked into her eyes.

'I'm fine,' she reassured him.

'You look quite pale,' he said slowly, his eyes roaming over her face.

'I was... I was worried about you.'

'How long have I been out?'

'Half an hour. I was putting a cold compress on your head but then I thought I might give you hypothermia because it's so cold anyway!'

He raised a hand and touched the bruise on his temple, wincing as he did so. But he smiled ruefully at her, touched her cheek gently and said ruefully, 'Thanks. I feel like a bloody idiot,' he added drily, pushing himself up. 'I was driving far too fast—well, let's see if we can get this show on the road.'

Somehow he did get the Land Rover going again and they limped home at a very sedate pace.

'Look, are you sure you're all right?' she said anxiously again as they came into the warmth of the kitchen and he flung the keys on the table. 'You look terrible now.'

'Nothing a couple of aspirin, a cup of tea and a good night's sleep won't help. What's this?' He took a piece of fine Swiss cotton, white with little blue flowers on it, out of her hands and held it up.

'Oh. It's my half-petticoat. It was the only thing I could think of to use as a compress.'

His lips quirked. 'Very... Lucy,' he said. 'Is it part of a matching set by any chance?'

'As a matter of fact, it is,' she said slowly.

'I thought it might be—don't look like that.'

'How am I looking?' she asked uncertainly.

'As if you're not sure whether to subject me to another lecture on the impropriety of discussing your underwear or—something else.' And for once his eyes held a sober, direct enquiry.

Lucy blushed, to her chagrin, then heard herself say gruffly, 'If you're sure there's nothing more I can do to help, I think I'll go to bed.'

'Nothing—I think that would be a good idea,' he said with a certain irony but, curiously, she couldn't tell if it was directed at her or him, and her confusion caused her to murmur goodnight and leave rather precipitately.

But as she lay in bed listening to him moving around the adjoining room—and then deep silence—the turmoil in her heart and the bereft feeling she experienced didn't make for a peaceful night.

And for the next few days the fact that he was not in a good mood at all didn't help.

'It's his head,' Adrian said philosophically when he'd received a cool, sharp set-down over something very minor.

'Yes, it's his head,' Shirley agreed with adoring overtones that caused Lucy to grimace.

'Well, I don't know why he doesn't take his head to the doctor,' she said, forgetting for the moment how concerned she'd been over Justin Waite's head.

'I'm sure it's nothing serious, Miss Lucy,' Shirley said very seriously. 'But a bump like that can give you a headache for a couple of days. I'll think up something extra nice for him for dinner!'

'Well, I think I'll keep out of his way for a while,' Adrian remarked, causing Lucy to grin this time and utter a similar sentiment, but this was something she didn't prove successful in.

Nor was the confrontation she finally had with him helped by her feelings of uncertainty and restlessness, the new awareness that she'd fallen in love with him up against the old awareness that he didn't love her...

It started when Sasha came to lunch two days after the accident. Justin was looking much better but he still had the bruise on his temple, which prompted Sasha to make enquiries, not unnaturally, Lucy supposed.

Justin explained briefly and then was called away to the phone as they sat down to a meal of soup and quiche.

'I hope you're looking after your man, Lucy,' Sasha said archly with her soup spoon poised but a highly unfriendly little glint in her green eyes at the same time.

Lucy raised an eyebrow. 'What makes you think I wouldn't?' she countered coolly.

'Why, nothing,' Sasha murmured. 'It was just one of those things one says. But, come to think of it, the last time I saw you two together you were, well, not in the greatest harmony, shall we say?'

Lucy gritted her teeth. 'That has nothing to do with you, Sasha.'

'Oops! Sorry,' the other girl murmured. 'Now I've upset you,' she added blandly.

'I'll tell you what should upset *you*,' Lucy retorted, 'is the fact that you wouldn't have the courage to say things like that if Justin were here.'

'Courage to say what?' Justin enquired coldly as he re-entered the room.

There was a short silence then Lucy said, 'Nothing.'

'If you two are squabbling,' he said sardonically, 'would you mind cutting it out? Sasha, we have quite a lot to discuss, so I'd appreciate it if you turned your mind to the business of the upcoming yearling sales.'

Sasha actually blushed, but Lucy smiled sweetly at her, turned an equally sweet smile upon her husband although she was thinking that she must be mad to feel herself in love with him, and said in a grave, hushed voice, 'We're suitably squashed, Justin. You don't feel we ought to write out a hundred lines after lunch? Do not squabble, do not squabble—that kind of thing?'

His mouth tightened and his eyes were very grey and hard as they rested on her. He also said with the kind of precision that would have cut through a steel plate, 'You're not very long out of school, are you, Lucy?'

If Sasha hadn't been there she might have poured her soup all over him, although what she did do was nearly as bad. She clanked her spoon down but said meditatively, 'I don't know why, but I seem to have lost my appetite, so why don't I leave you two to have a very adult discussion—yes, because to be honest, both of you *grown-ups* bore me to tears. Have fun!' And she got up and walked as lightly as she was capable of out of the room.

But when Justin found her in the stables ten minutes later, there were real tears streaked down her face, tears of anger and anguish as she employed a pitchfork with considerable energy to lay down new hay in an empty stall.

It was his tall shadow that fell across the floor of the stall that first alerted her to his presence and she stopped what she was doing, turned to him and said brightly but witheringly, 'Finished already? That *was* quick.'

'Lucy——' he reached over to take the pitchfork from her '—no.' And as she resisted, added curtly, 'Don't be an idiot, you'll only get hurt waving that thing about.'

Whereupon she resisted even harder, but after an un-dignified, quite unequal little struggle he wrested it from her and leant it against the wall. So she glared at him, stalked past him and plonked herself down on a bale of hay. 'All right, go ahead! I'm sure you've come to tell me how childish I am again.'

'I haven't, as a matter of fact, but I did warn you once, Lucy, that you could fight me all you liked in private, but in public—it would be a different matter.'

'Fight you!' she marvelled with magnificent scorn. 'You started it! And I'll tell you something, Justin Waite—I don't enjoy fighting in public either but I will *not* put up with being insulted *in* public. You're only lucky you didn't cop a bowl of soup.'

'For someone who doesn't enjoy it you seem to in-dulge in it fairly frequently,' he said drily.

'Only when I'm provoked,' Lucy said proudly. '"If you two are squabbling..."' she repeated. 'Who do you think you are?' she added intensely. 'If you really want a wife then you better start treating me like one.'

'And if, Lucy,' he drawled, 'I were treating you like a *wife*, this wouldn't keep happening.' Then he added with a relaxed little smile suddenly playing around his mouth, 'But I have to give you full marks for sheer spirit and courage. I'm also beginning to wonder how your father ever coped with you, not to mention your school.'

Lucy stared at him then whispered suddenly, 'I hate you, Justin. I was mad to think anything... any-thing——' She stopped abruptly.

'Anything...?' He raised an eyebrow.

'*Nothing.*' She got up, but found he was barring her way. She looked up at him for a long, tense moment, then her shoulders slumped suddenly and she said wearily, 'What now?'

'What *did* she say to you?'

Lucy's lips parted. 'Do you mean...?'

'I mean Sasha.' He lifted a hand and traced a tear streak down her face then kept his fingers on her chin.

Several emotions chased through Lucy's eyes but finally she said with simple dignity, 'I'm not going to tell you, Justin. I was quite capable of dealing with it on my own.'

'Until I stuck my oar in?' he suggested, looking wry.

'Yes,' she said pointedly.

'Something to do with the fact that we—don't always get on?' he hazarded.

But Lucy refused to speak, although her pansy-blue gaze did not attempt to evade his and after a long moment he laughed softly, kissed her lightly on the lips and released her chin. 'Such a proud, stubborn little wife. For what it's worth, I've sent Sasha back to Riverbend with a lecture.'

Lucy's eyes widened. 'Why?'

'Why?' He grimaced. 'You are my wife, while she is only my assistant.'

'If that's the case, why did you——?' She stopped and frowned bewilderedly up at him.

'Why did I say those fatal words in the first place? About squabbling?' He paused and shrugged. 'Well, Lucy, I have to be honest and confess to you that there are times when it's not easy—*playing* at being a husband,' he said with a significant little look up and down her figure.

A slow tide of colour started to travel up the line of her throat. 'Is that... is that why you've been in such a bad mood?' she whispered, her eyes wide. 'Not your head?'

'Well my head hasn't helped,' he said amusedly.

'I didn't...I didn't realise,' she said confusedly. 'But now I do, I don't quite know what to do about it. I can't...just suddenly...come to bed with you,' she said agitatedly. 'Only a moment ago I was quite sure I hated you!'

'And now, a moment later?' he queried with a wicked little glint in his eyes.

'I haven't entirely forgiven you yet; I may still feel quite annoyed even to think about it for a time!'

He looked down at her with something in his eyes she couldn't read, something that made her feel very young, though, and realise the total irrationality of what she'd said, and she closed her eyes suddenly in a fever of embarrassment.

'Then why don't we approach things from a different angle for a while?'

Her lashes lifted and she frowned up at him. 'What do you mean?'

'We began this week in a kind of harmony; let's just try to get back to that,' he said seriously but his grey eyes were amused again.

'All right,' Lucy replied slowly.

'Good.' He took her hand. 'Shall we finish our lunch now? I don't know about you, but I'm starving.'

CHAPTER FIVE

SO THAT was what they did, and once again their household started to shape up in a rather jolly way.

Adrian spent a few hours each day in the vegetable garden and the chicken house, repairing the damage he'd wreaked, and was rewarded for his efforts each day with a flight over the property or a tractor ride or just being allowed to accompany Justin. Lucy again took part in these expeditions and Shirley, seeing more contentment in her son than she'd ever seen, probably, cleaned and polished, washed and ironed and cooked up delicious meals. She even began to lose her agitated look.

But Lucy was hauntingly conscious that it couldn't go on like this forever, that she would have to make some decision soon, and confess to herself that, her own feelings aside, these glimpses of what harmony with Justin and Dalkeith could be like were nearly irresistible. Where did all my hostility go? she wondered once, and felt her cheeks burn as she remembered the rash thought that she could somehow make him regret marrying her, and another even rasher thought—the crazy idea that she might enslave Justin Waite—only to end up the one who was enslaved herself... What she would have done once that was accomplished was not quite clear, but that she should even have entertained it proved to her, now that she could think more clearly, that being really married to him had never been so unthinkable. Indeed, perhaps at the back of her mind there had always been a fatal fascination about it.

I think I must have always been a little in love with him, she mused painfully, and all that anger was caused more by hurt pride than by anything else, because he doesn't love me the same way. What would be worse, she wondered: to be married to a man you hated or married to a man you loved who didn't love you? And even if you did decide to live with it, how did you take that final step...?

It was ironic thus that what in the end did help her should also be the cause of Justin Waite's not loving her as she believed she loved him... She had thrown Joanna Madden's name at him once—their relationship had after all been long-lasting and well-documented. Come to think of it, Joanna's was the only name Justin had been linked with like that... Then, out of the blue, Joanna had married an older man who was very wealthy and twice divorced. But what Lucy had not expected was to meet Joanna Madden in the flesh and at Riverbend.

They'd taken Adrian and Shirley to see the yearlings that so soon would be going to the sales—Shirley in quite a flutter of excitement because this was her first flight. They'd not alerted Sasha other than buzzing the stud office, which was Justin's way of saying he was arriving, and they'd arrived. There was another light plane on the runway which Justin had stared at with a frown—the Maddens'. And they'd all met up in the stud office with Sasha looking pink and confused and as if she couldn't believe this was happening to her.

'Oh, Justin,' she said as he walked over the doorstep, 'I...um...the Cawnpore filly...that is Mr Madden here...is very interested in her breeding and he called me up on the HF and said they were flying over Riverbend and asked if he could take a look...'

'That's no problem, Sasha,' Justin said smoothly as his grey gaze swept the room and took in the couple standing across it. 'Joanna, Tim, how are you? I don't know if you've met Lucy?'

Joanna Madden, Lucy decided a bit dazedly as there was a slight pause, was still lovely. About thirty, she was dark, tall and graceful and she had an air that marked her as a person of inner grace—she had had it when Lucy had met her briefly years before but now it had another quality that was hard to define except to say that it was slightly haunting...

'Yes.' Joanna came forward, breaking the pause that had begun to stretch. 'We did meet once, Lucy; I don't know if you remember? Tim,' she turned to her husband, who looked to be in his early fifties but was tall and spare, 'this is Lucy Wainright from Dalkeith, Justin's next-door neighbour.'

This time the pause was crashing. Sasha actually closed her eyes before Justin said quietly, 'In fact Lucy and I got married a couple of months ago, Joanna.'

Joanna's eyes jerked to his, but that was the only sign she gave that this news might be momentous, because the next moment she murmured, 'We've been overseas for so long! Oh, I do wish you both every happiness. *We* do, don't we, Tim?' And she turned to him and slipped her hand into his.

'Justin?'

'Mmm...?'

It was that same evening and, as they'd got into the habit of, they were sitting in the library after dinner. It was raining again.

'I think you should tell me about Joanna Madden, Justin,' Lucy said.

He stretched his legs and looked into the fire for a while. 'What do you want to know?'

'Why she didn't marry you. Why she looks...sort of sad. Why she couldn't hide for a moment what a surprise it was that we'd got married. And why, considering past history, her husband should even consider taking her to Riverbend, let alone buying the Cawnpore filly.'

He turned his gaze to her at last. 'Taking things unchronologically, Lucy, that Cawnpore filly is the best of the bunch. She shows signs of wonderful conformation, she has marvellous bloodlines on the distaff side—so much so that I've put a reserve price on her even Tim Madden might find hard to fork out.' He looked towards the fire again and his gaze was extremely meditative.

Lucy was briefly diverted. 'If that's the case, why are you even contemplating selling her?' she queried.

After a long moment he shrugged. 'I own her dam and her grandam and——' he gestured '—Cawnpore. He was a gamble but he's proving himself as a sire now, so you could say I'm on a bet to nothing. It's all still there at Riverbend, the genes. Not that everything is ever a certainty, but then again, I could keep the filly and race her and have her break down on me or a hundred other things go wrong with her—it happens. It happens all the time with horses. I've hung on to what I've thought were the best before, only to find it wasn't so.'

'But mares—well, fillies,' Lucy protested, 'even if they don't race well——'

'They can be barren, they can run into fences, they can get colic. I think too,' he frowned, 'that while I would have liked to retain an interest in her if I didn't have her dam and grandam, I see myself essentially as a breeder. Racing horses is another game in a sense.'

Lucy stared at him. 'All right. I guess I can see the logic in that,' she said slowly. 'But why would Tim Madden want her? From you, I mean.'

Justin smiled faintly. 'Tim is a racing man above all else. Horses are a subject that transcend everything with him.'

'Even to putting his wife through—an experience like that?'

Justin didn't move but he transferred a slightly wry grey gaze to her. 'What makes you think it was such an experience? Joanna and I broke up two years ago.'

Lucy hesitated then she said simply, 'Why?'

She thought he wasn't going to answer so she then said, 'I'm not asking this because I want to poke or pry——'

'Don't you?' He raised an eyebrow at her.

'No,' she insisted a little heatedly. 'But my intuition tells me it could have something to do with why you married *me*. So why should I be kept in the dark?' She lifted her chin defiantly at him.

He smiled again, idly and as if at some inner thought. 'Very well. Joanna discovered she was unable to have children.'

Lucy felt her eyes widening and had to stop herself from staring at him open-mouthed as well. 'So she wouldn't marry you and—and married a man who already had a family. Justin! Oh—how terribly sad!'

'Now don't get all carried away, Lucy. It's not nearly as dramatic as you make it sound.'

'But it must have been! When two people really love each other——'

'That's fairy-tale stuff you're talking, Lucy,' he said drily.

'But she looked so—haunted for a moment or two!'

He said nothing, and his expression was indecipherable as he looked into the fire until Lucy said, 'And you've never forgiven her, Justin, have you?'

He looked up then and said impatiently, 'Of course I have. The sadness you see in her is probably to do with not being able to have anyone's children.'

'I—well—Justin——' Lucy looked at him confusedly '—I don't know about that but are you sure you didn't marry me because it didn't matter much to you who you married after—her?'

'Lucy,' his lips twisted and his eyes were suddenly amused, 'if that were the case, that I married simply for the sake of it, don't you think I would have found myself a much more *compliant* candidate for a wife?'

Lucy's brow creased. 'I suppose so, but don't forget they didn't have the other half of Dalkeith.'

'That's true,' he said wryly. 'So you're unique in several senses.'

She tightened her mouth. 'I also very much resent being married because it's so *practical*,' she said bitterly. 'That's what you said to me!'

'My apologies,' he replied gravely. 'If I'd put it to you that we'd once been good friends, how would that have affected you?'

'I'd have probably liked it better,' she said but grudgingly.

'Would you have admitted it, though?'

She opened her mouth, closed it and reddened. Then she said haughtily, 'I don't know what point you're trying to make, Justin, it's quite lost on me. But the point I'm trying to make is that we're locked in a loveless marriage—and I'm beginning to see why!'

'Lucy,' he said evenly, 'I've never denied the practicalities of our marriage. But its lovelessness hasn't been put to the test yet. I've told you that from my point of view it's a commitment, not some nine-day wonder, and I mean that. When you try it, you'll see what I mean.' He stood up and stretched. 'And here endeth that lesson, but perhaps I could say one thing more. Romance and moonlight and declarations of never-ending love are all very well—indeed, I wouldn't expect you to live without them entirely.' He smiled down at her unexpectedly and added wryly, 'Not you. But there's a whole lot more to it, as many a romantically inclined girl has discovered to her cost. So don't be too scathing about practicalities; they often build into something strong and enduring *because* they have a basis to build up.'

Lucy's lips parted and she frowned. 'Why not me?'

He lifted a lazy eyebrow. 'Why not you what?'

'Why wouldn't you expect me of *all* people—you didn't say that but you might as well have—to live without—well, all those things *you* were being scathing about?'

His lips twisted. 'Are you not the Lucy Wainright about whom some bloke flew a plane over Sydney Harbour trailing a banner asking you to marry him?'

Lucy's eyes sparkled with indignation. 'I don't think it's fair to blame me for that! I'd given him absolutely no cause to imagine I would!'

He grimaced. 'Perhaps not. I do remember the papers writing you up as rather heartless because you declined.' He grinned. 'Still, some very romantic gestures have come your way, you must admit.'

'They did,' she said with youthful dignity and a very steady gaze from her pansy-blue eyes. 'It may have escaped you that I didn't take any of them up, Justin. No one rushed me into marriage because of moonlight and roses. You were the one who did the rushing.'

'You're only twenty,' he said mildly, ignoring the rest of her speech.

'I may be, but I'm not entirely a fool.' She stood up herself. 'I'll have to think about *this* revelation now! I hope you have no objection to that?'

He took his time replying. He studied her brave stance and her outfit of grey cords and a lovely chunky grey and white sweater. His gaze lingered on her loose hair and finally her face and there was something in it that caused her to catch her breath slightly and be suddenly aware of him differently, something undoubtedly admiring in his eyes; it was as if they were a man and a woman caught in a moment of intimate curiosity. *No*, she thought, as a sensation that was becoming familiar coursed through her body, a sensation of leaping pulses and trembling anticipation. He can't do this to me. Not when he's just told me about Joanna! And she switched her gaze away confusedly.

'By all means, Lucy,' he merely said after a moment.

She turned away and walked towards the door, praying he wouldn't guess what an effort it was to appear completely normal.

Yet despite that puzzling look, over the next few days Lucy couldn't help feeling that Justin was withdrawn and preoccupied, in fact he spent a lot of time at Riverbend, much to Adrian's disgust.

And she couldn't help wondering how much that unexpected encounter with Joanna had affected him. It also occurred to her that he had never denied being in love with Joanna. And she thought to herself often, it's all falling into place, isn't it? It has to be. You don't marry someone the way he married me unless there's a reason like that behind it. So what do I do now?

It also struck her as unfair that during those few days she could settle to nothing because of a curiously bereft feeling...

What she did do was quite unexpected, as it happened, and it all boiled up one evening out of the blue...

She was sitting at the piano playing Chopin when Justin came in—she hadn't seen him for two days and he'd arrived after dinner, which Shirley had kept warm for him, and elected to eat in the kitchen where Adrian had regaled him with *his* doings of the past few days.

Lucy had stayed for a while then wandered into the library and started to play softly. She looked up now as he closed the door, and felt her heart contract. He was wearing jeans and a black sweater and there were marks of weariness on his face beneath his ruffled dark hair and something drained and moody in his eyes. He also said briefly, 'What's wrong?'

'Nothing. I ... I was going to ask you the same.'

'Why?'

She played a chord quietly. 'I thought you looked— tired and disenchanted, that's all.'

He shrugged. 'I am tired. A consignment of twenty-five yearlings to break in and get ready for a sale is a tiring business.' He sat down in an armchair and lay back. 'Play some more,' he suggested after a minute or so. 'How come you play so well?'

'Mother Angelica, at school,' Lucy said with a grimace. 'She used to tie me to the piano stool—no, not really, but she was a very determined person, and eventually I grew to love it.'

'She was your music teacher?'

'She was much more than that,' Lucy said wryly. 'My headmistress, the bane of my life often, yet, looking back, rather wise and someone I'll always admire.'

He said no more, so she played, and noticed out of the corner of her eye that his hand on the arm of the chair clenched and stretched a few times, then relaxed. What she didn't notice was the way he watched her straight back, the sweep of her eyelashes as she concentrated, how she sometimes, as a lovely melody evolved beneath her fingers, bit her bottom lip.

She also found herself thinking about Mother Angelica as she played, that hard-headed but wise nun who had had very clear ideas on a whole host of subjects including the role of wifedom that would come to most of her charges...

And she must have played for nearly an hour with those thoughts on her mind, until she began to wonder if he'd fallen asleep, but, as she closed the piano softly and stood up, she saw that he had not.

'Sorry,' he said, and grimaced. 'I'm not great company tonight, am I? That was very...relaxing.'

Lucy hesitated then sat down opposite him. 'Strange to say,' she said very slowly, 'I'm sorry I can't offer you the more conventional form of relaxation wives are supposed to provide—but I don't think it would help to try to be a substitute tonight—do you?'

She saw his mouth harden briefly then thought he might have forced himself to relax as he drawled, 'So that's what's bothering you—Joanna again.'

'Yes,' she admitted composedly, 'but it may surprise you to know all my thoughts on the subject.'

He lifted one black brow wryly. 'Well, go on, surprise me.'

She looked down and smoothed the fabric of the long tartan skirt she wore with a dark green angora cardigan that had little pearl buttons. Her hair was tied back simply with a matching green ribbon. And she answered obliquely, 'Do you...could you believe that I think domesticity is overtaking me, Justin?'

He narrowed his eyes. 'I think you'll have to explain a bit better than that, Lucy.'

'I...I just have it in me at the moment to believe I could be quite a good wife, to be modest and industrious—you're probably going to laugh——'

'No,' he said slowly with a frown in his eyes. 'But when did all this hit you?'

When you walked in tonight, she answered in her heart, and when I thought of Mother Angelica, that's when it all crystallised, but she said, 'Over the last few days, I suppose.'

'Well——' He paused and watched her searchingly. 'What are you suggesting?'

'That's up to you, really. I mean——' she hesitated '—if you still feel we could make a go of it.'

'I've never changed my mind about that. Lucy——' he paused '—you're not about to sacrifice yourself on the altar of your no doubt highly dramatised version of what happened with Joanna, are you?'

'Not while she's still so close to you,' she said, and thought he swore under his breath but made herself go on bravely, 'and not that, no. Just—well, you yourself told me it comes to most people, a time when they have to make the best of things, so...that.' And she lifted her chin and stared into his eyes with dignity.

He swore properly this time and said roughly, 'Do you know how old you look, Lucy? About sixteen.'

She flinched. And said honestly, 'I feel a lot older than sixteen, Justin. I know how young I must appear to you but right now I feel like a woman for the first time in my life probably.' She stopped awkwardly and licked her lips nervously as she sought to explain what was in her heart. 'And I'm beginning to understand what my options are, I guess. Go away from here, or try to build something worthwhile with you. And I suppose it came to me that if I'd had the courage to go away, I would have done it at the beginning. It's also come to me that even if you couldn't love me as you did Joanna, if you did care all the same, then you're right, there is something to work on.'

'What if,' he said very quietly, and she thought she saw a tinge of pain in his eyes, 'my...the way I love you doesn't come up to expectations?'

'You mean if I really fall in love with you but it doesn't happen the same way for you?' She stopped, but he didn't answer or make any gesture so she said, 'Then

I'll have to pour it all into Dalkeith, and you'll have to give me some children, Justin. But there's one thing I've got to tell you before you make up your mind.' She hesitated, then took a deep breath. 'It's one of the reasons why making this decision has been so difficult for me— I don't know if you'll believe this but I'm not very experienced about lovemaking. In point of fact...I've never actually done it.'

'I know——'

'Now if that alters *your* decision I'd quite understand. I mean it's a bit different for two reasons at least—you *what*?' She stared at him with her lips parted and her eyes huge.

'I know that you're a virgin, Lucy.'

'But how can you possibly—know?' she whispered.

'Because your innocence in these matters—shines like a lamp,' he said with irony, self-directed irony she thought, but such was her confusion that she didn't give it more than a passing thought.

'But everything you've *said*,' she protested, and bit her lip.

His lips twisted. 'It suited me to—go along with everything *you* said with such bravado, my dear. I also——' he paused and regarded her crestfallen countenance with something unusually gentle in his eyes '—have known you for a long time and always had quite a bit of respect for you, Lucy.'

'Respect,' she murmured dazedly. 'But what about——' she licked her lips '—what about getting a proposal of marriage from a plane over Sydney Harbour? And, I did have—well, quite a few boyfriends, although——' her eyes flashed suddenly '—I certainly deny "queening" it over all and sundry!'

'My apologies. In fact you were a sight for sore eyes when you were—in full flight. Is that a better way of putting it? But still quite obviously a lovely, laughing girl who had given herself to no one.'

'Oh.' Lucy groaned and put her hands to her hot cheeks. 'This is so humiliating!'

'On the contrary, it's something to be proud of.'

'So you married me—you don't mind, in other words?'

'Why should I mind?' He smiled faintly.

'Well, I could turn out to be frigid for one thing,' she said starkly. 'And isn't it a little bit different—taking someone untouched into a marriage like this, other than someone who might have a better idea of... all sorts of things!' She eyed him indignantly.

He sat up abruptly. 'You're not frigid, Lucy.'

'That sounds so essentially male!'

'It may be,' he said with a tinge of impatience, 'but believe me, it's true.'

'Do all men know so much about women?' she asked then with turmoil and confusion showing in her eyes.

He shrugged. 'I don't know. And you're only one young woman we're talking about. I don't claim ultimate wisdom on the subject. All it means is that I'm quite a few years older and have a lot more experience.'

She stared at him for a long moment, then said, barely audibly, 'Do you know what I wish? I can't help wishing at this moment,' she whispered desolately, 'that I were planning to be a modest, industrious wife to someone who didn't necessarily have any experience but who loved me so much that it wouldn't matter.'

'Strangely enough,' he answered very quietly, 'at this moment, so do I.'

'Justin——'

But he stood up and walked over to her and held out his hand. 'Lucy—you could still take my other offer. You talked of an annulment once...' He paused as she put her hand into his uncertainly, and pulled her gently to her feet. 'If that's really what you want to do,' he finished.

She didn't realise the leap of fright that showed in her eyes, but she did make herself say, 'Because you saw Joanna again, is...is that——'

'Lucy, that's over and done with,' he said grimly. 'I——'

But she wouldn't let him go on. Speaking from a deep well of fear in her heart, she said haltingly, 'Well, perhaps if you can't have her and I can't have—an imaginary person who might never exist anyway, could we console each other, do you think?'

It was his turn to stare down into her eyes with something like real regret in his, until he said, 'We could try.'

'Well——'

She got no further, because he put a finger to her lips and murmured, 'I think we've probably said as much as one can say on the subject. I think the time has come now to—let things take their course. Like this.' And he took her into his arms and started to kiss her.

It was quite some time later when his mouth left hers and she discovered that just about everything else had left her mind, Joanna Madden included, because it seemed she was wholly focused on Justin Waite and the rapture his lips and his hands had inflicted on her body and imprinted on her soul. It was also a revelation because she hadn't expected it, yet this kiss couldn't have been more different from the only other time he'd kissed her, and that was what she'd expected—another give-nothing-away experience. And it was what she'd expected to bestow, she realised shakily. But she'd received and bestowed far more, and her breathing was undoubtedly erratic as she stared up at him, not wanting to be released. Heady again with the feel and the taste of him but completely abandoned to it this time, her skin trembling finely in anticipation as his hands wandered down her back and found the gap between her cardigan and skirt and lingered on her waist, then slipped beneath the elastic waistband of the skirt and slid down to her hips, scantily clad in a tiny pair of fine silk bikini briefs.

Her breath jolted in a little flare of shock and his eyes narrowed as he saw it, but the shock waned almost as quickly as it had flared, and she came unresistingly as he pulled her even closer because there seemed to be a current flowing between them, or from him to her, she thought, a sort of sensual pull that both amazed her and filled her with an inner quivering that was a mixture of longing and excitement—and the knowledge that she wanted to be nowhere else on earth but in Justin Waite's arms.

It was like a compulsion such as she'd never known, and an awareness that made her drink in everything about him, the way his dark hair fell and those little lines beside his eyes—they weren't creased in amusement, she noted, in fact his eyelids were half lowered in a rather intent way and he seemed to be watching her mouth with interest, just her lips, which sent another tremor through her as she remembered how his own had explored the soft skin of her neck and a little further down when he'd flicked open a couple of little pearl buttons...

And she made a helpless little sound because it was also terribly unfair that he could make her feel like this, though of course, to be perfectly honest, it had been growing in her for a long time, hadn't it? It had probably been there when she was fourteen and measuring up her very first date at the school dance...

'And what is going through your mind at the moment, Lucy,' he said very softly and kissed the corner of her mouth chastely.

'I still think we should wait until...'

'No, now,' he said and took her back into his arms. 'This has gone on long enough, and it will be all right, I promise you.'

'Justin,' she whispered, her colour fluctuating, her breathing erratic, 'do you mean...?'

'Yes, now, tonight.' And stopped anything further she might have said by kissing her.

'I feel—I feel so different,' she said later.

'Do you?' Justin drew his hand down her pale, slender body and rested his dark head on his hand so he could look into her eyes. There was one lamp on in her bedroom and the bed was rumpled, the fire now low. 'Tell me.'

'I feel translated somehow.' Her voice was low and husky. 'Does that sound odd to you?'

'Not at all.' He stroked her cheek. 'I feel a bit that way myself. You're incredibly lovely, you know.'

'But was I any good?' she said very quietly. There were faint blue shadows beneath her eyes, her hair was damp and disordered and there was something young and bewildered in her eyes, as if she couldn't quite believe what had happened, couldn't quite make the transition to having him lean and strong, dark and naked in bed beside her.

He smiled and pushed some golden strands of hair off her face. 'You were tender and—delicious. Didn't you notice my reaction, incidentally?'

She thought for a moment and closed her eyes at the memory of the feel of his hard body on hers and how he'd made her want everything he'd done to her, how he'd made her feel soft and smooth and told her she was like a work of art—how there'd been no pain at all, how her eyes had opened and her hands on his back had fallen slack and she'd gasped as sheer pleasure had risen in waves through her body and she'd felt the convulsion of his with a sweet sense of triumph.

'And you came yourself, didn't you?' he said as all this passed through her mind.

'I . . . yes, something happened to me that was quite wonderful,' she confessed.

'Then——' he pulled up the sheet and held her close '—all is well.'

But she said seriously, 'Justin, I just have this feeling I may have given myself away and I'm a little worried about it, you see.'

He moved his chin on her hair and she thought he laughed softly. 'Given yourself away how, Lucy?'

'Let you know that I do love you——'

'You don't have to worry about that.'

She grimaced. 'I suppose you knew that too all the time I was—pretending to myself. But what I'm worried about is that it might be a burden to you so——'

'No, Lucy——' he put his fingers to her lips '—it's not, it never can be, so don't say any more. Let's just relax and be happy. Go to sleep, in other words, my sweet, talkative wife,' he said wryly, and kissed her brow.

Lucy subsided, although part of her wanted to have it out with him, but the rest of her couldn't help but feel warm and safe, and it was so lovely lying against him and feeling his hand stroking her back that she ended up falling asleep before she knew it.

And morning brought her some reassurance.

She woke to find him watching her with something unmistakably tender in his eyes. He also said, 'How do you feel, Mrs Waite?'

Her lips curved. 'Fine, thank you, Mr Waite.'

'Then would you mind—if I did this?' And he drew the covers aside and touched her nipples until they started to unfurl and a sense of longing travelled down her body, and her eyes widened in such surprise that he laughed and kissed her. 'Don't look like that, it's quite normal to wake up feeling sexy. I've been doing battle with it for about half an hour.' And he eased his weight on to her gently.

They showered together afterwards and she ate a huge breakfast then went for a ride, during which, for the first time since their marriage, she told him about some of her ideas for Dalkeith and he listened attentively and with approval. But after lunch he said he had some work to do so she, somewhat to her surprise, found a book and curled up with it for the whole afternoon.

'Lucy?'

She looked up to see Justin standing over her with something wry in his eyes.

'Hi!'

'I wondered where you were—the place was so quiet.'

She stretched and yawned and closed the book then glanced at her watch and blinked in surprise. 'It's nearly dinnertime! Is this what being married does to one?' she asked with a glint of humour.

'There's no sin in it,' he replied, helping her up and kissing the top of her head.

'It seems very slothful, however,' she commented, and leant against him.

'Perhaps that's what honeymoons were designed for.'

'Oh! Perhaps you're right!' She glinted a smile up at him. 'To help new brides get over the shock of it all.'

'Shock?' he queried tilting her chin up and with something quizzical in his expression.

'What I mean is——'

'Did it come as such a shock, Lucy?'

'No, not really.' She lowered her lashes. 'But something has to account for the fact that I seem to be——' she paused '—in a state of suspended animation at the moment,' she said thoughtfully. 'I mean, after all the weeks of trauma, it's finally happened—you'd think I'd at least be analysing it, turning it over and over, trying to poke holes in it—that sort of thing, instead of peacefully reading a book all afternoon. Oh, no!' And she looked up at him with a curiously comical, wide-eyed look of horror.

'Lucy, you've got me seriously worried,' he said wryly. 'Oh, no what?'

'I've just remembered something you said to me!'

'Well, tell me.' He fingered the collar of her blouse and his lips twisted. 'Before I die of curiosity.'

'I don't think I should—you'll be able to say I told you so! And I don't think I'd appreciate that one bit...'

He grimaced. 'I can see I'm going to have to use strong-arm tactics, Mrs Waite. Shall we go up to our bedroom?'

'What do you mean?' She was genuinely wide-eyed now.

'Just that I could kiss you there until you were happy to confide in me without the possibility of Adrian or Shirley stumbling upon us, and just in case it went— further than that.' His grey eyes were entirely grave.

'That's...incredible blackmail, Justin!'

'I know but one of much the nicest forms of it you'd probably find.'

'Then I'll spike your guns here and now, sir,' she said and started to laugh. 'It's just that you did say to me once that without regular, satisfying sex I could get troublesome and fractious——'

'Actually I said *women*——'

'It was still an amazingly superior kind of thing to say, whether you were generalising or being particular, or so I thought. Now I have to wonder if you were right, which is rather demoralising actually——'

'Then perhaps this will help,' he interrupted. 'From now on, without regular, satisfying sex with you, Lucy, I'm the one who could become fractious and troublesome.'

She stared up into his eyes and was so totally intrigued and fascinated by this possibility, she forgot to say anything at all.

Until he said softly, 'What deep, dark plans are you concocting for me now, Lucy Waite?'

'Nothing!' But she blushed and got hotter as he laughed quietly and kissed her on the lips, and said, 'If it weren't for the fact that dinner *is* only ten minutes away...' But he didn't go on as they heard Shirley come into the dining-room next door; instead he raised a rueful eyebrow—and Lucy breathed a tiny sigh of relief.

It was after dinner that he brought up the subject of honeymoons again.

'You know,' he said as they sat down before the library fire, as it was raining again, 'once the yearling sales are over we should take our delayed honeymoon. Where would you like to go?'

They were sitting side by side on the settee and Lucy raised her hands above her head and said, 'Oh—the Seychelles, where I could get around in a bikini all the time and if it rains it's warm. Or—Tahiti sounds nice, Justin,' she said, parodying a television advertisement with a pert look.

'It does indeed, but seriously——'

Her expression grew serious. 'Closer to home? I don't mind—that didn't sound very modest or industrious, did it?'

He laughed quietly and pulled her onto his lap. 'The thought of you in a bikini all the time in the Seychelles is seriously electrifying, all the same. What I was going to say was, do you have a *serious* desire to see them or were you teasing me?'

She considered for a moment then all of a sudden found herself with tears in her eyes.

'What's the matter?' He frowned down at her.

'I don't know—how very embarrassing! I think being in a position *to* tease you, Justin, is something of a revelation and... and...' She couldn't go on.

'Lucy,' he said quietly and stroked her hair, 'this is only reaction—it has all been pretty traumatic but it's *over* now.'

Lucy laughed shakily, and Adrian stuck his head around the door. 'Mum's looking for you two.'

Justin stilled Lucy's sudden movement. 'Ask your mum if we can have our coffee in here, Adrian. Is something wrong?'

Adrian advanced into the room and continued his critical study of them from close quarters. 'She sick?' he asked at last.

'No. Just tired,' Justin said gravely.

'Didn't know you two felt like that about each other,' he said with the extreme unselfconsciousness of youth and because he was Adrian anyway, and extremely perceptive with it.

'As you see, we do. I hope you approve?' Justin enquired.

Adrian shrugged. 'Don't know much about it. I haven't got a father so my Mum doesn't go in for it.'

'Yes, well, that could change one day, Adrian, and if it does I'll tell you how to handle it. The best way is to ignore it and leave them in peace.'

Adrian considered. 'OK,' he said at length. 'I reckon I get the message. I'll tell Mum to knock like the clappers when she brings the coffee and not to rush it.'

'You're a bright boy, Adrian,' Justin said with not a breath of laughter. 'In fact I'll add to that, I reckon you'll go a long way.'

'Thanks,' Adrian replied off-handedly. 'By the way, I've changed my mind. Not sure about being a farmer any more. I think I'll be a pilot. See you later.' He withdrew and closed the door behind him.

But Lucy could contain herself no longer. She began to laugh uncontrollably and felt Justin's iron control give way too. 'Oh, God, he's a character, isn't he?' she gasped.

'One of the best.'

It was minutes before they were quiet again, although Lucy was still subject to the odd breathless little chuckle.

'Feeling better?' he asked.

'Mmm.' She moved her cheek against his chest and thought how warm and safe she felt and how she'd like to stay like this all night. And as the thought took possession of her mind, she raised her lashes and whispered, 'I can, can't I?'

'Can what?'

'I'm just thinking aloud; it doesn't matter.'

'Yes, it does.' He put his fingers under her chin and made her look up at him.

'I can spend the night with you—that's what I was thinking, that's all,' she said, and shrugged and coloured all at the same time. 'You're probably wondering if I've gone feeble-minded,' she added ruefully.

He laughed quietly—and then swore as the phone rang.

It was Sasha with the news that the Cawnpore filly had severe colic.

'I'll have to go—Lucy, I'm sorry,' Justin said intensely.

'But it's dark and it's raining, Justin, and you——'

He sat down and took her hands. 'It's stopped raining and it's clear over Riverbend, and I have an instrument rating for night flying—Lucy, that filly could bring a hell of a lot of money at the sales if we can save her and I don't have to tell you that colic can be fatal in a horse. I have to go, much as I hate to.'

Her hands quivered in his but she said, 'Of course. Good luck with her. Will you ring me when you arrive?'

'Yes.' He leant forward and kissed her. 'Sleep well, Mrs Waite.'

'I'll try...'

She was actually in bed although not asleep when the phone rang, but it was Sasha to say that Justin had arrived safely, and that they looked as if they had a difficult night ahead of them and not to expect him home until tomorrow.

Lucy replaced the receiver and regarded it balefully for a moment. 'I don't know why I put up with that woman,' she also murmured. 'Only she could, in the space of a few short sentences, contrive to make me feel quite useless while she's being so strong and competent,' she marvelled.

She put the lamp out with a snap and slid down to curl up beneath the covers in her pink and white polka-dot silk pyjamas. Then it occurred to her to wonder what Sasha and the rest of the world would make of the latest development in the Waite marriage, assuming they'd been privy to what had gone before—which they hadn't, she reminded herself, but might have sensed or guessed it.

But her overriding emotion, she discovered, was a hauntingly new feeling of vulnerability. Because I'm alone? she asked herself. I didn't feel like this earlier today, I felt serene and—well, *happy*. She grimaced suddenly and tried to think back over what had happened and how it had happened but, as she'd found all day, it all seemed dreamlike and not susceptible to analysis...

It was as if all she could think of now was how much she loved Justin Waite, and how, oddly, that had opened up a whole new field of vulnerability for her.

She fell asleep with it on her mind.

CHAPTER SIX

LUCY woke up to a warm, clear morning the next day and a call from Justin this time, to say that the filly was responding to treatment but still not out of danger, and he'd have to stay with her until she was.

'Of course,' Lucy said down the line. 'I quite understand.'

'What will you do?'

'As a very new wife who's lost her husband on the second day of her—well, what should be her honeymoon?' she said with a chuckle. 'I'm not altogether sure, Justin.'

'Lucy——'

'No—I'm only teasing, I really am fine,' she said wryly, and they chatted for a few minutes more. And when she put the phone down she discovered she did feel a lot better, with none of the shadows of the night before lurking in her mind, and after helping Shirley during the morning she had lunch then saddled her horse and went for a ride.

It was such a pleasure, after all the rain they'd had, to be out in warmth and sunshine, that she actually found herself singing as she rode along. She also thought wryly that she was exhibiting classic symptoms of being in love—and that just a few words from Justin this morning had achieved a minor miracle.

It was quite unwittingly that she rode towards the twelve-mile paddock, which true to form could be more accurately described as a bog in parts. Any more rain and it would flood as it often did, she thought and paused to breathe in the air and the sky and take off a jumper as she let her horse pick its way. And since she'd got this far, she decided to check the repairs to the old boundary riders' hut.

The hut could not even by a long stretch of imagination be described as anything but rough and ready but the roof and door had been repaired, a supply of firewood laid in for the stove as well as some basic provisions and there were new mattresses on the two bunks and some heavy duty blankets that resembled horse blankets in texture. She grimaced as she felt them then raised her head suddenly as she realised that in the half-hour or so she'd been poking around the afternoon had gone curiously still. And the fine hairs on her body stood up in the eerie silence which was broken, as she swung open the door, by a sheet of lightning that filled the sky and an enormous clap of thunder that caused her to jump about a foot in the air. What was worse was the fright her horse got, which caused it to rear and whinny and break its lead, and, on discovering itself free, show her a clean pair of heels as it headed for home.

'Oh, no!' The words were torn from her as the sun went out in a manner of speaking and the first raindrops fell like bullets from an enormous thunderhead and more thunder and lightning split the sky.

But it was 'oh, yes'; she was marooned, the twelve-mile was bound to flood with this storm; she should have realised the unusual warmth in the air could lead to storms and she'd told nobody where she was going...

'Well, I'm quite safe,' she told herself as she closed the hut door against the uproar outside, 'it's just that nobody knows it. And it did come up so fast; anyone could have been caught napping—well, anyone with other things to think of. Could I be blamed for this? Not really,' she reassured herself, resolutely stilling the slight niggle of her conscience by adding, 'All's well that ends well, don't they say?'

It was nine o'clock before it finally stopped raining, but there was still thunder in the air, and, when she peered out, an obliging flash of lightning illuminated an eerie scene—water lying everywhere below the high ground the hut was built on, more water than she'd ever seen in the twelve-mile, probably waist-deep in some parts, she guessed, and she shivered as she remembered her grandfather telling her about a flash-flood that had swept through the paddock once and lapped the door of the hut. So she closed the door and concentrated on the fact that she was dry and safe. In fact it was quite cheerful inside the little hut. She had a roaring fire going in the stove, she'd eaten a dinner of baked beans and biscuits and there was a pot of coffee bubbling away. She'd also pulled the two mattresses off the bunks and put them on the floor in front of the stove—it was now very cold, and a wind was getting up which would probably blow the storms away—good news really, although the danger of flash-flooding still depended on how much water was draining into the paddock.

It was probably due to the rising wind and the crackle of the fire that she heard nothing as she sat huddled on a mattress under one of those hairy blankets and sipped her coffee. In fact her first intimation that she was not alone came when the hut door opened precipitately, nearly blew off its hinges and a tall, dripping figure stood there.

She nearly died at the unexpectedness of it, spilt her coffee and yelped with pain then gasped as she put her cup down. 'Justin! You frightened the life out of me! Couldn't you have knocked——?'

But with a swift lunging movement her muddy, torn and tattered husband hauled her to her feet and grated through his teeth, 'What the *hell* are you doing here, Lucy? Have you no sense at all? Just how long are you going to be a giddy, thoughtless, brainless eternal schoolgirl?'

If he'd just not said those last words, the short fuse to her own temper might not have lit, but it did in a blinding flash because she knew she was no longer a schoolgirl or giddy or thoughtless and brainless, in fact she knew she was a woman in just about every sense of the word with a lot of the heartache that seemed to go with the condition—and all at his hands. So she wrestled an arm free, spat at him, 'I *hate* you, Justin Waite! I wouldn't *be* here if it weren't for you.' And she hit him hard and accurately on his cheekbone.

His grey eyes blazed beneath his dark, dripping hair, and his mouth twisted in a frighteningly savage way, then he jerked her into his arms, stared briefly into her widening eyes, darkening with fright as her face paled, and started to kiss her ruthlessly.

She sagged to her knees when he let her go at last, her heart pounding, her mouth bruised and her whole body shaking.

He stared down at her for a moment, their eyes locking, then he said grimly, 'Don't you realise that every able man on the place is out searching for you, that we've even called in the State Emergency Services helicopter?'

She gasped. 'I... but there was no way I could let you know I was all right. My horse b-bolted, you see——' her teeth chattered '—it was the thunder, then it started to pour—it was really all just... one of those things,' she finished helplessly in a bare little whisper, and dropped her head into her hands.

'No, it wasn't,' he said precisely. 'It was a case of plain thoughtlessness, Lucy, and in future don't you ever go galloping off into the blue without telling someone *where* you're going. Do you understand?'

'Yes. Look, I'm sorry——'

But he cut her off. 'And for someone who knows as much as you do, or claims you do, to come *here* when you know the history of this bloody paddock was sheer lunacy. Look at me, Lucy,' he commanded.

She did, and could have cried because of course he was right. If only she hadn't been so happily pre-occupied! But she refused to allow herself the luxury of tears. 'You're right,' she said in a stiff little voice. 'I was extremely stupid. I won't do it again. How did you get here?'

His mouth set in a hard line then he pulled off his oilskin. 'I drove as far as I could then I walked and finally I swam.' His eyes glinted with mockery and she winced. 'I just hope,' he continued, pulling a two-way radio wrapped in more oilskin out from under his shirt, 'this survived the experience.'

It had, and she breathed a sigh of relief as he called off the search, thanked everybody, and it was decided they'd be safe for the rest of the night and a rescue attempt would be made in the morning.

'We'll bring a boat this time,' the voice on the other end promised with more good-naturedness than one would have expected.

But it didn't appear to improve Justin's humour. He put the radio down, glanced at her coldly then started to remove the rest of his wrecked, sodden clothes.

Lucy took a breath, wondered incredulously if she was being sent to Coventry, but some impulse made her guard against putting it to the test immediately. And she turned away and busied herself.

'Here,' she said after a while, and handed him a cup of steaming packet soup. There was a pot of canned braised beef simmering on the stove and she'd hung his clothes over the bunks. He'd stripped to his underpants and was wrapped in a blanket. She'd earlier found a coarse old towel and he'd rubbed himself down with it and the muscles of his shoulders and thighs had rippled under his fire-bronzed skin.

He took the soup and drank it in silence then started on the beef, and all he said was, 'Aren't you having any?'

'I'm not hungry—I had something earlier.'

He didn't reply and she busied herself at the rudimentary sink which was a bucket on a table, and wondered how long it would be before she was considered suitably chastened and worthy of talking to.

He finished the coffee she poured for him and lay back with his hands behind his head. She hesitated, then sat down cross-legged on the other mattress half turned away from him and sipped her own.

And she nearly spilt another lot of coffee as he said suddenly, 'Would you care to explain, Lucy, why you wouldn't be here if it weren't for me?'

'I—what I meant was,' she said carefully, 'that I had some things on my mind. And so I wasn't quite as—um——'

'On the ball as you should have been,' he completed for her drily. 'That's no excuse.'

'Well——'

'Lucy,' he said dangerously.

She grimaced and sipped some coffee. 'Perhaps you're right.'

'Perhaps?'

'All right,' she said quietly. 'I've admitted it was stupid, *I* am stupid——'

'All the more so if those things you had on your mind,' he said sardonically, 'are to do with us.'

She took a breath. 'I can't quite agree with you there, Justin.'

He swore beneath his breath and turned to look at her, resting his head on one hand and then for reasons she couldn't fathom, he swore again but added in less abrasive tones, 'For what it's worth, I don't usually go around kissing little girls quite as brutally as that.'

Involuntarily, Lucy raised a hand to her mouth, and she said a little foolishly because she couldn't think of anything else to say, 'I'm glad. It's a bit—well——' She paused, then hastened to say, 'I don't usually go around slapping people's faces either, but I did think you'd done me an injustice, you see. I still do.' She paused and looked at him resolutely, then she said, 'What I didn't take into account at the time was all you'd been through. Could we both have been just a bit at fault?'

Justin Waite stared at her expressionlessly and she was entirely unaware that the firelight enhanced the gold of her hair, deepened the blue of her eyes, had brought a delicate flush to her cheeks so that she looked troubled but almost ethereally lovely. Nor did she understand why he closed his eyes briefly and sighed as he said, 'What injustice, Lucy?'

'Well I'm not just a little girl, I'm your wife for one thing and what I meant about—not being here if it wasn't for you—was the simple but awkward fact that . . . that I was in a bit of a love-struck daze and *that's* why I wasn't completely on the ball,' she said in a rush. 'But now I can't help wondering when you're really going to start treating me like a wife, Justin. Maybe one who makes mistakes occasionally but who doesn't deserve to be treated like a child.'

His expression hadn't altered during her speech and all he said at the end of it was, 'Come here, Lucy.'

Her eyes widened. 'Why?'

He raised a wry eyebrow. 'So I can start treating you like a wife—why else?'

But a defiant little spark lit her eyes. 'If you think that's all it's going to take——'

'Yes, I do,' he interrupted. 'It's a time-honoured custom between men and women——'

'But I think it should be *said*,' she objected.

'As a matter of fact, this will probably say a lot more than either of us could say in words—let me show you.' And he knelt up and reached for her and when she made a convulsive movement he sighed quietly but didn't release her and said abruptly, 'Trust me for once, Lucy.'

She looked up into his eyes and blinked away the tears she was still determined not to shed. And the faintest smile touched his mouth as he observed the tilt of her chin and he said, 'All right, I apologise. But when you've been wondering whether the body of your wife is going to float past you, it tends to—well, as you saw. Do you think you could see your way clear to allowing yourself to be undressed now?'

She licked her lips and her pulses started to beat erratically. 'Well—only if you'll allow me to say that I seriously regret hitting you.'

'Thank you,' he said gravely and pulled her sweater over her head then removed her blouse, and with her help, her jeans so that all she wore in the glow of the fire was a navy blue bra with little white flowers on it and matching briefs.

'Very—fetching,' he murmured.

'They're French,' she confided, sitting on her heels, her hands on her thighs.

'There's one thing I can think of that would be prettier than you in them—and that's you out of them.'

She laughed then sobered as she gazed at him. 'You're—I have to tell you I think you're quite magnificent, you know,' she said huskily. 'Just in case you thought I wasn't affected or something like that. Indeed, the truth is, I'm quite seriously affected.'

'Lucy——' he reached behind her and released her bra '—any more words along those lines and I'm liable to become uncontrollable.'

'Well, that I can't imagine,' she said, and caught her breath as he touched her naked breasts, and she lifted her hand, not sure what she wanted to do, but he caught it and raised it to his lips and kissed the palm.

'Firelight becomes you,' he murmured, turning his attention back to her nipples until they unfurled. And he stroked all the soft, silky places of her body—her armpits, the back of her neck, the curve of her waist, but each time returning to weigh her full, high breasts that quivered on the slender stem of her body like luscious fruit. Until she could stand it no more and she leant forward and slipped her arms around his neck and laid her brow on his shoulder and said his name pleadingly.

She woke slowly to a dim grey light filtering into the hut. And she made a contented little sound and closed her eyes again, but then her lashes flew up and she was staring at close range into Justin's eyes. She blinked and other things intruded upon her consciousness, that she was nestled in his arms, that they were covered by two scratchy horse blankets—and it all came back to her and her eyes widened.

'It's all right,' he said softly, and raised a hand to brush her hair off her cheek.

Lucy relaxed and said with a little sigh, 'This is terribly nice, you know. Even here.'

'I'm glad,' he replied, his lips twisting slightly. 'It is for me too. I take it I'm quite forgiven?'

'Of course,' she said. 'I thought I'd made that obvious last night.'

'Well, you did let me make love to you last night,' he said thoughtfully.

Lucy's eyes widened. 'Wasn't that enough? I also apologised for hitting you...'

'So you did. I was only wondering whether I had sufficiently apologised for kissing you the way I did.'

Lucy took a breath and looked at him earnestly but with a trace of shyness. 'To be honest I'd forgotten all about it, and if that didn't show—well, don't forget I haven't done this often.'

He smiled rather quizzically down at her. 'All the same you do it with a lot of style.'

She forgot to feel shy. 'Do I really? In what way?'

He moved the blankets aside leisurely and his grey gaze skimmed her body. 'Well, there's the way you move, the things you say—and sometimes the things you don't say, but I can read them in your eyes all the same.'

She grimaced. 'I had the feeling I was a dead giveaway.'

'There's nothing to regret in that. It's very appealing. And there's the way you're lying here discussing this so gravely with me, with not a stitch of clothing on—believe me, that's intensely appealing, speaking as a man,' he said seriously but with laughter lurking in his eyes.

Lucy blushed but laughed a little herself. 'Speaking as a woman, you're tremendously appealing, I have to say, Justin.' And she put her hands on his shoulders tentatively.

'Go on.'

Her lips quivered and she moved her hands across his shoulders. 'Well, you're tall, dark and handsome for one thing—I did tell you that last night. You can be very nice at times, for another. I must say it's also very reassuring to have you around, yes, even when you're cross with me,' she said airily. 'Let me see,' she continued, 'you——'

'Lucy,' he interupted, 'you're teasing me.'

She opened her eyes very wide. 'I wouldn't dare!'

'Oh, yes, you would. But I have to tell you I have the perfect solution for pert girls.'

'You do?' She frowned. 'Let me guess.' And she leant forward so her breasts brushed against his chest and kissed him lightly on the lips. 'Something along these lines?' she asked with her eyes dancing wickedly.

'Precisely. You're learning very fast, my dear.'

She laughed and rested against him. 'I think I couldn't have a better teacher. Justin—are you asking me to make love to you again? Because, if so, it would be a pleasure...what's the matter? Is something wrong?' she queried anxiously as he moved suddenly then swore.

'Depends on which way you look at it.' He grimaced. 'But I think I can hear our rescuers approaching. Does that sound like an outboard motor to you?'

She listened then sat up abruptly. 'Yes!'

His lips twisted. 'Well, it's not cause for alarm but they're bloody early.'

Lucy scrambled up. 'You better put some clothes on.' And she gathered an armful of his clothes, felt them anxiously then handed them to him. 'They're pretty dry.'

He sat up more leisurely. 'So they are. There is no stigma attached to being caught in bed with your husband, Lucy.'

She cast him a rueful look as she started to dress hurriedly herself. 'I know, but...'

'You think there is?' He drew on his shirt and pushed the other blanket aside. Then he stood up with his shirt still unbuttoned and the hut seemed to shrink.

'No stigma, no,' she said, 'of course not——'

'The lady doth protest too much, methinks,' he said wryly, and caught her hand. 'Tell me, Lucy.'

She stared up at him and for a moment forgot entirely what she was going to say as she studied the blue shadows on his jaw, his dishevelled hair and decided he looked younger this way, and that she rather liked it...

'Lucy?'

'Oh.' She bit her lip and coloured. 'Sorry—what was I saying?'

'Nothing,' he replied amusedly, 'but you were looking—perturbed about being caught in bed with me.'

'Ah, that—um...' she said, dragging her mind away from her thoughts with difficulty. 'Even married couples probably don't relish being caught in bed.'

'True,' he agreed gravely, buttoning his shirt and reaching for his mud-stiffened trousers. 'But there are probably a lot of people out there who were wondering when we were going to take up our marital bed.'

Several expressions chased through her eyes before a look of indignation took hold. 'I know, but it has nothing whatsoever to do with them!'

'True again,' he murmured, and looked with disfavour at the thick jumper he'd worn under his oilskin. 'That doesn't usually stop people wondering.'

'I'm quite sure Sasha for one,' Lucy said with considerable hauteur. 'If you must know, Justin, it will give me a lot of pleasure to... demonstrate otherwise to her.'

He grinned and pulled the jumper over his head. 'That doesn't seem terribly consistent with your desire to get up out of our bed a few minutes ago, Lucy.'

She thought for a moment then tossed her head and smiled mischievously up at him, 'Well, you see, Justin, there's a difference. Being caught in bed, even with my legally wedded spouse, by a boatload of grinning, knowing men would quite possibly have rendered me all blushing and coy. Whereas dropping the odd subtle hint to Sasha would not.'

'Lucy.' He laughed and caught her again as she went to go past him and took her chin in his hand,

'Yes, Justin?' she said demurely.

'Don't change, will you?' he said after a moment but she got the oddest feeling he'd been about to say something else. He also added wryly, 'They're here.'

They were, and the news they brought with them was not good. Not only was the twelve-mile flooded, but the whole property was in danger of inundation.

'Please, Justin, let me help!'

'Lucy——'

'You can keep an eye on me. You can give me orders as you do to the others. I promise you I'll obey them to the letter!'

He raised a wry eyebrow. 'That would be a new experience but all the same, Lucy——'

'Justin.' She put a tentative hand on his sleeve and tried to mask the hurt in her eyes. 'Don't leave me out. I love Dalkeith, and to sit by and watch this happening, to know that stock are drowning and so on, is more than I can bear. You said yourself you need all the help you can get—and I can ride as well as any of them!'

'Lucy.' He paused and stared down into her eyes. 'I know that. But there are some things you won't want to see, some things you won't be able to do.'

'Perhaps,' she conceded, 'but there must be some things I *can* do. Please.'

He hesitated. 'All right—but I have to say this: if you become a liability at all, if we have to divert someone to look after *you*—well we just can't afford the manpower.'

'You won't,' she said quietly.

She was as good as her word and for the next week, as the floodwaters peaked then started to recede, she spent every daylight hour in the saddle, herding wet, bedraggled sheep from one soggy paddock to another. And she fell into bed every night exhausted. She noted though that she was never allowed to work on her own and, as Justin had predicted, there were sights she wished she hadn't to see. But she never flinched other than inwardly or turned away.

Once, during the week, Justin who had not only Dalkeith but Riverbend to worry about and divided his time between the two, although by a freak of nature Riverbend wasn't as badly affected, stopped her as she was about to set out at the crack of dawn, and inspected her face intently. 'How are you?' he queried.

'Fine!'

'Don't overdo it, Lucy,' he warned.

'I'm not. You must be worried sick about the year-lings and the foals.'

'I've got all the yearlings out. And so far we haven't lost a mare or a foal but it's touch and go. Look, are you sure——'

'Quite sure,' she said quietly but firmly.

He narrowed his eyes then smiled unexpectedly. 'They tell me you've been as good as any bloke on the job.'

It was what kept her going, those words of praise. But finally the day came when the crisis was past and she walked into the kitchen late in the afternoon, knowing she wouldn't be needed the next day.

Shirley fluttered about her anxiously as she sat down at the kitchen table. 'Oh, look at you, Miss Lucy, you've been doing too much! You're only a slip of a girl——'

'No, I haven't,' Lucy protested, and stood up again, but her knees buckled unexpectedly and if Justin hadn't come through the door, she'd have fallen.

'Lucy,' he said grimly through his teeth as he picked her up. 'I warned you!'

'But I helped, didn't I?' she whispered, and closed her eyes.

His expression softened slightly. 'You were a bloody marvel,' he said. 'But one day you're going to learn to really do as you're told.'

'You were the marvel,' she said huskily. 'If you hadn't been here to co-ordinate it all...' She shivered and didn't seem able to stop, and buried her face in his sweater.

'Shirley,' he said over his shoulder, 'in about an hour, could you bring our dinner upstairs?' And he shouldered his way out of the kitchen with Lucy in his arms.

'I'm fine really,' Lucy said as he set her on her feet.

'So I see,' he commented as he started stripping her clothes off. 'Lift up your arms.'

Lucy obeyed, and he removed her pink vest, which left her standing in her bra and jeans, the fact of which she seemed unaware as her brow creased. 'It hasn't been a total disaster, has it? I know we lost some but we saved plenty too...Justin,' she said on a sudden jolt of breath, as she realised he was releasing her bra, 'no...'

Their eyes locked for an instant and her cheeks started to burn but he continued what he was doing saying quietly, 'This is a bit strange, Lucy. Not that I can blame you for wondering when we're ever going to be at leisure to consummate our marriage properly but—I have done it before. And all I intend to do at the moment is inspect you from top to toe. Seven days in the saddle is tough on most people.'

'You're right, I don't know what got into me,' she said breathlessly. 'Is there any chance of the Seychelles?'

He laughed and kissed the top of her head. 'Unfortunately the blasted Yearling Sales are almost upon us.'

An hour later she was ensconced in bed in her pink and white polka-dot pyjamas, and Shirley had brought up dinner for them both, and was unfurling napkins and fussing around them.

'We'll be fine, thanks, Shirley,' Justin said eventually.

'Well, if you need anything just give me a call!'

Justin looked expressively at Lucy as she left but he said, 'I've had a thought. How would you feel about taking Shirley on permanently?'

Lucy blinked. 'I think it would be great, but would she want to stay?'

He laughed. 'Would she ever? Not only does she worship the ground you walk on, but the son of her heart is a reformed person. I'm sure she would. She'd be close to her aunts as well and Adrian could enrol in the School of the Air with the rest of the property kids. I get the feeling it might be hard to tear Adrian away, anyway.'

'I think he worships the ground you walk on,' Lucy commented.

He shrugged and said. 'Eat up, Lucy. We don't want you wasting away.'

She picked up her knife and fork. 'I don't think there's the least danger of that——'

'You certainly felt a few pounds lighter.'

Lucy ate some roast beef in silence.

'What's wrong?' he said after a minute or so.

'I don't know,' she replied, her brow creasing as she put her knife and fork together. 'Well, yes, I do, although it's a little hard to put into words.'

'I think you'd better try,' he said with a smile in his eyes.

'Would you...would you come to bed with me? Now? Not to... well, whatever you like, but I'm just feeling a little shell-shocked, sort of, and I think I need some help.'

Ten minutes later, when he'd got rid of their dinner plates and she was lying in his arms, he said, 'Feeling better?'

'Oh...yes,' she whispered with a relieved sigh. 'Sorry.'

'Don't be. You did far too much but, be that as it may, will you come to Sydney with me for the sales?'

'I'd love to,' she said huskily. 'Would I be in the way, though?'

'Of course not. You might even be a considerable asset. There's an enormous amount of socialising that goes on. You could also, much enamoured as I am of your French underwear, collect yourself a trousseau, meet old friends—have a break, in other words.'

But Lucy, much to her embarrassment when he reminded her of it the next morning, was fast asleep.

'Right. I have a few things to do—why don't you hit the shops, Lucy?'

'I will, in a while,' she replied over her shoulder as she completed a tour of the downstairs area of Justin's townhouse in a fashionable inner suburb of Sydney. 'I love it!' she added enthusiastically, looking out over the tiny courtyard. The living area was furnished mainly in subtle beiges and sandy pinks with sandstone walls, wooden-framed windows and multi-paned French doors with brass knobs. There were big comfortable chairs covered in ivory fabric and the dining table was clear glass and forged iron tinted a soft, old green.

'I'm glad,' he said gravely. 'It's yours to command.'

'Oh, I won't change a thing!'

His lips twisted. But he said, 'By the way, we've been invited to a cocktail party this evening. It's a pre-sales do. Would you care to accompany me, Mrs Waite?'

'I'd be delighted to, Mr Waite,' she said grandly.

He smiled but his eyes were faintly probing as they rested on her face. 'You're very chipper, Lucy.'

'Why shouldn't I be?' She eyed him innocently.

'You've just been through a rather harrowing experience, my dear,' he said after a moment.

'I recover quickly,' she said ruefully. 'You really don't have to worry about me.'

'Sometimes the effect of these things can be—more insidious than one realises. And I can't help thinking you have a look about you of the kind of high spirits that give way to tears before bedtime.'

She swallowed suddenly and hoped he didn't notice. Because of course he was right in a way. Her high spirits were a front for a little spring of tension that had hit her rather suddenly because on the flight from Dalkeith, it had begun to dawn on her that she and her marriage to Justin Waite were going to be very much on show over the next few days. But she was curiously loath to let him divine this. So she said with a laughing look, 'I got over that kind of thing when I was about ten, Justin,' she said with a laughing look. 'I'm just a naturally ebullient kind of person.'

'I see. All right.' He looked her over narrowly once more then shrugged. 'I'll be back at five, we're due at the party at six. In the meantime, these are for you.' He drew his hand out of his pocket and held it out to her. In it was a key-ring, a wad of money and a bank card.

Her eyes widened and she licked her lips. 'I... Justin, you don't have to——'

He picked up her hand and closed it over the contents of his. 'Of course I do,' he said lightly. 'You can't shop without money, you need transport and you need the keys of the house. Go ahead and enjoy it.' And he kissed her briefly on the top of her head and walked out.

She got back to the townhouse at three o'clock, parked the racy little sports car that was apparently hers in the double garage, and carried quite a few packages into the house. But only one of them contained clothes, the rest holding food. A quick tour of the pantry before she'd left had shown her that it was bare. She'd also bought a percolator, the one bit of equipment the kitchen didn't seem to have, and before long the aroma of coffee was drifting through the house. And she took her mug with her as she made a more detailed inspection. There were three bedrooms upstairs, the main one done out in white and yellow and overlooking the courtyard. She opened the linen closet and discovered it packed with thick, thirsty towels and matching linen sheets and pillow cases, some of them not even out of their wrappers.

And the impression that this house wasn't used a lot was reinforced when she checked the china cupboards and discovered glasses and cutlery still in their boxes. She grimaced and wondered who had bought it all. Perhaps he'd got an interior decorating firm in, she surmised, and they'd supplied it. Or perhaps... But she closed the door of her mind on that thought at the same time as she closed cupboard doors, and thought instead, resolutely, well, whoever did it, it's *nice*.

* * *

She was dressed and almost ready when she heard the front door open and close, and she looked over the banister and called out that she'd be down in a tick.

'No hurry,' he called back. 'I've got to get changed yet—is that coffee I smell?'

'Yes, it's on the stove.'

They met as she was halfway down the stairs and he was starting to come up.

'Hi!' she said gaily as he stopped with his foot on the bottom step. 'How was your day?'

'Lucy...'

'Are you lost for words? I do hope not in a *disapproving* way.'

He moved away and said wryly, 'Come right down and I'll be able to give you a proper evaluation.'

She hesitated briefly, although she wasn't sure why, then continued down and went to stand in the middle of the room.

'Turn round,' he said.

She did so obediently, then looked up at him gravely. 'Short skirts are in, Justin.'

He said nothing as his gaze flickered over her again. She wore a midnight-blue Thai silk suit. The jacket was short and fitted into her waist with a wide collar that exposed her throat and the tops of her shoulders and the sleeves were elbow-length. The straight little skirt came to six inches above the knee and she wore very pale frosted stockings and high-heeled blue shoes that matched the outfit. Her hair was piled on top of her head with some curly strands framing her face.

'What do you think?' she asked at last, unable to stand the suspense and quite unable to read his expression.

'I think,' he said expressionlessly then smiled faintly as her eyes grew anxious, 'that you look simply stunning, my dear. And that I shall have to watch out in case any susceptible blokes out there take to flying banners over the harbour again.'

Lucy relaxed and had to laugh. 'I quite thought you didn't like it!'

'Why wouldn't I?'

She gestured. 'I wasn't sure it was a terribly—modest, wifely outfit, somehow.'

'But you chose to wear it all the same?'

'Don't you think it is?' She looked at him seriously.

'Not at all. I didn't say that. And wives are allowed to look stunning. Husbands are usually quite keen on that, in fact.'

'Then why do I get the feeling you don't entirely approve?' she said slowly.

'I don't know—why do you?' he countered.

'Well,' she frowned up at him, 'you did—sort of stop when you first saw me.'

'Ah. So I did. But that's easy to explain. I was simply bowled over, particularly by your legs.'

Lucy's eyes widened and then her lips curved into a smile. 'Thanks,' she said huskily. 'I needed that.'

'Lucy,' his lips twisted, 'it's true—you would be able to bowl a block of wood over. Hell——' he looked at his watch '—I'd better get moving. By the way, I see you did the grocery shopping. Thanks. I always forget.'

'You don't have to thank me; that's what wives are for, especially industrious ones,' she said, but distractedly. 'Aren't they?'

A wicked little smile lit his grey eyes. 'Among other things. I'll be about ten minutes.'

* * *

Lucy drew a deep breath and Justin looked down at her with a faint frown. 'Something wrong?'

They were just about to enter the cocktail party venue, she could hear the buzz of voices and clink of glasses, but she paused and realised she had a vaguely uneasy feeling at the pit of her stomach.

'Lucy?'

'Um—I'm fine, Justin,' she said with a glance at him. But that made things worse, she discovered. He wore a grey suit with a pale blue shirt and navy blue tie and he looked both worldly and enigmatic, tall, broad-shouldered and incredibly attractive—and way out of my league? she enquired of herself with a little sigh.

'Are you feeling sick or something?' he asked with a frown in his eyes.

'No,' she said uncertainly. 'Well, not really. But it's just occurred to me that there could be four people here who know about me handcuffing kids to fences, let alone telling you I hate you. And that the whole of Sydney might now know of it! And, much as I hate to admit it, my stomach is doing strange things right now and I'm not terribly sure that I can... do this.'

'Lucy——'

'Justin——'

'No, Lucy, listen to me.' He took her hand and turned her away from the double doors, at the same time as he gestured to a passing waiter carrying a tray of glasses, and after a short enquiry relieved him of one that contained neat brandy. 'Here, have a sip of this.' He handed her the glass but didn't release her other hand.

'It might make me sick...'

'No, it won't,' he said positively. 'It'll settle your nerves.'

She looked up at him out of huge eyes and with her lips trembling, but he pressed her fingers gently, and she raised the glass to her lips and took a sip, and then several more. Then she shuddered, but as the fiery warmth made its way down to her stomach she felt herself steadying. 'You're right,' she said blinking several times.

'I'm quite often right,' he replied wryly.

'All the same——' a frown creased her brow and she looked anxiously past him '—it——'

'Lucy—I've told you this before but it's true—I don't give a damn about what other people think and neither should you. This is between us and it's all over anyway. But in point of fact, you do know what most people will be thinking? That if I couldn't make you happy, I must be out of my mind. In other words——' his lips twisted '—it's me they'll be wondering about, not you.'

Her lips parted. 'If they do,' she whispered, 'they also must be wondering if you're still in love with Joanna Madden—don't you see?'

'No, that's over and done with,' he said firmly, his grey gaze as steady as a rock. 'Now, we can do one of two things. We can go home if you still don't feel up to this and it won't worry me in the slightest. Or we can go in there—and give them something else to talk about.' He smiled unexpectedly.

'Wh-what?' she stammered.

'Well, should you choose never to leave my side—that kind of thing—they might very well say to themselves that Justin Waite is doing it right at last.' He stared down into her bemused eyes and grimaced slightly, but he added, 'Why don't we try it?'

CHAPTER SEVEN

WHICH was how it came about that for the first time in her life Lucy Waite née Wainright had an attentive escort who was also her husband. And it was a revelation. She wasn't quite sure how he did it but he somehow contrived to make her feel special, as if he were as interested in her as if not more so than anyone else they met. Nor did he give her the opportunity to stray from his side even if she'd wanted to. And she couldn't help noticing that they were the centre of quite some attention.

It's incredibly heady, she thought a little dizzily at one stage, as she stood beside him and glanced up to see him watching her with a faint smile on his lips and a look in his eyes that was exclusively for her, a look that contrived to make her feel ravishing and *interesting* and of singular importance to him. Also to see the envy in other women's eyes as they looked at him, particularly Sasha, who had come forward to meet them as soon as they'd entered, and stayed glued to their side ever since.

Yes, well, Lucy thought privately, as Sasha, who was dressed in mint-green that went well with her red hair, moved restlessly, perhaps you won't be quite so superior with me now?

And she had almost decided to let herself just be happy—she'd certainly got over her bout of nerves and was laughing at something someone was saying to her—when she looked across the room and straight into Joanna Madden's lovely, haunting eyes. And that was

when it all collapsed like a pricked balloon. It was no
coincidence that their eyes had caught, she knew that in
her bones. Joanna had been looking at her for some
moments, she was sure, and didn't seem to be able to
look away either, so that it was Lucy who did. And, as
she did, it crossed her mind to wonder whether what
Justin had said about "giving them something else to
talk about" might have been directed more at one particular person?

'Lucy?'

'Oh, sorry, Justin,' she said a few minutes later. 'Did
I miss something?'

He looked her over thoughtfully. 'No. But enough is
enough, I think. Shall we go home?'

She could only nod gratefully.

'Why don't you change into something more comfortable
while I make us a snack?'

'I'm not hungry, Justin, but thanks all the same.'

'Lucy——' he caught her hand as she went to walk
past him '—do it.'

A spark of rebellion lit her eyes. 'Why should I?'

'Because you'll make yourself sick if you don't eat,'
he murmured with nothing other than a slight tinge of
amusement in his eyes. 'I only had a sandwich in mind,
and coffee.'

Her shoulders slumped. 'OK.'

He let her hand go but his gaze held hers. Then he
smiled absently and turned away.

She changed into a creamy satin nightgown and a white
towelling robe and sighed as she let her hair down,
brushed it then tied it back in a simple pony-tail. For
reasons she didn't think had much to do with her ex-

ertions at Dalkeith, she felt really tired and dispirited—
in fact she knew the reason all too well, she chided
herself, Joanna Madden—is she going to haunt me
forever? she wondered. Why can't I just take what I've
got and make the best of it? I shouldn't have come, she
thought finally, I'm OK at Dalkeith but this is like being
on a rollercoaster ride... How am I going to be now,
for instance?

When she got downstairs, Justin had laid out his
supper on an occasional table and drawn it up to a settee.
There were open toasted cheese sandwiches, a bowl of
fruit and a fresh pot of coffee.

'Mmm. Smells nice,' she said very mundanely. 'I didn't
know you were a cook.'

He grimaced. He'd taken off his jacket and loosened
his tie. 'A very ordinary cook. Sit down.' He indicated
the settee. 'Would you like to listen to some music?'

'Yes, please.' Lucy sat down and watched him glance
through a pile of compact discs. Then moments later
some lovely guitar music flooded the room. He turned
it down and came to sit next to her.

'Help yourself,' he murmured. 'It's cheese or cheese.'

'I like toasted cheese,' Lucy heard herself say, and
wondered why she should be feeling unwittingly soothed.
The music? The fact that Justin had gone to the trouble
of making this snack? She grimaced.

'Something wrong?'

'No!' she denied hastily, and concentrated on eating
her sandwich. When she'd finished he peeled and quar-
tered an apple for her and poured the coffee.

'Tell me what else you bought today?'

She cradled her mug in her hands and tucked her feet
under her. 'I bought an outfit to wear tomorrow to the

sales, a dress for the ball you mentioned tomorrow night, and that's all.'

He raised an eyebrow. 'Is that all you intend to buy?'

'I don't know. One has to be in the mood.'

'How does one get into the mood?'

'I don't think one can consciously do that—you either are or you aren't.'

'So events outside you are the telling factor,' he commented.

She wrinkled her nose. 'Probably.'

'Is that to say if you were feeling happy and confident you would go out and splurge?'

Lucy considered with a faint smile. 'It could be the other way around; sometimes people do things like that when they're down in the dumps and need cheering up.'

He drank some coffee then sat back with his arm along the back of the settee. 'What I'm trying to get at,' he said after a while, 'is which of those states you might be in.'

She turned her head to look at him and whispered one word. 'Why?'

'Why do I want to know? Why shouldn't I?'

'Sometimes I'm happy and confident, sometimes I'm not——' She stopped abruptly and put a hand to her mouth.

'For a little while this evening you were both.'

'Justin,' she said huskily, and to her consternation she felt tears in her eyes, 'I...it's not easy to...' She broke off frustratedly.

'There's one thing that makes it all much easier. Don't cry,' he said with a faint smile quirking his lips and he took her coffee cup from her. 'This.' And he took her into his arms.

'Justin!' she protested on a suddenly panicky note.

'There's nothing to be afraid of.'

'It's not that I'm *afraid* of anything.'

'Good,' he said wryly, and lifted her onto his lap. 'Then you should be able to relax.' And he did nothing more than hold her lightly and after a while it seemed only natural to rest her head against his shoulder rather than sit tensely upright against his arm.

Although she did say, challengingly, 'I am rather tired.'

'So am I. Cocktail parties can be an exhausting form of socialising and I'm not at all sure why people inflict them upon themselves.'

She smiled against his shirt. 'That's what my father used to say. Why stand around doing a juggling act with drinks and bits of food stuck on toothpicks when you have to shake hands with people all the time? He used to say it was a cheap form of entertaining.'

Justin laughed.

'How are the yearlings? Is that what you did today?'

'Yes. They all seemed to have settled in well.'

'Will they go under the hammer tomorrow?'

'Six tomorrow, the rest the next day.'

'I suppose Sasha has everything in hand?'

'Sasha has,' he agreed. 'With her usual superb efficiency. She is in fact being quite painful at the moment.'

'Justin!' Lucy beamed a marvelling blue gaze up at him. 'I never thought to hear you say that.'

He grimaced. 'I don't know why, but lately it's occurred to me that Sasha doesn't have a sense of humour.'

Lucy giggled. 'Poor Sasha.'

He looked down at her ruefully. 'You don't say that with a lot of feeling.'

'No, I don't,' Lucy replied unrepentantly. 'She makes me want to bite sometimes.'

He grinned. 'She probably envies you terribly.'

'I'm sure she does, but only over you... I mean...' She stopped and moved restlessly.

He stilled her movement and put his fingers under her chin so that she had to look into his eyes. '*I* meant,' he said quietly, 'that she envies how young and fresh you are, how lovely, how natural, how vibrant your personality is—those things.'

'Little to know if so,' Lucy whispered, 'what a trial some of those things are to me.'

Something flickered in his eyes. 'They shouldn't be. They aren't to me.'

Her lips parted and her eyes widened.

'In fact they're often the opposite,' he went on, releasing her chin and pushing some strands of hair off her face. And he bent his head and started to kiss her.

'Oh,' Lucy said breathlessly some minutes later. 'Oh.'

'May I take that as approval?' he murmured.

She swallowed and moved her cheek on his shirt and was unable to reply because the fact of the matter was, she was still unbearably affected by his kisses and she couldn't help thinking how ridiculous it had been to try to pretend to him that she was too tired for his lovemaking when she seriously doubted that would ever be the case...

'Lucy Waite?' he said gravely.

'Justin——' it came out rather cracked '—I can't talk. I know that sounds ridiculous and I'm sure you're aware that I'm talking right at this moment, but——'

'I am. Aware of it.'

'Well, it's not the same thing.'

His lips twisted. 'It's not?'

'No.'

'All right. Then let's devise a system of non-talking for those things that can't be talked about. If you would like me to kiss you again, you have only to nod your head.'

'I...'

But he waited no longer and it was the same wonderful experience, although this time he slipped his hand beneath her robe and slipped down the narrow strap of her nightgown. And, far from resisting, Lucy sighed with delight as she felt his fingers resting very gently on her breast.

'Nice?' he queried against the corner of her mouth.

'Lovely,' she breathed. 'I didn't know it could be so...'

'Didn't you?'

'Not until you did it to me—I feel a bit of a fool,' she said ruefully, but he took no notice and continued to touch her.

'Justin?' she said, because in spite of her delight she felt slightly chagrined, she found, and *young* as well as foolish. 'Is this doing anything for you, Justin?'

He'd been looking down at her in a curiously heavy-lidded way, but all of a sudden he stopped what he was doing and that heavy-lidded look changed to one of open amusement. 'Of course it is. I wouldn't be doing it otherwise,' he said wryly, and added, 'What is going through your mind at the moment, Lucy?' as he kissed the corner of her mouth chastely.

But she didn't want to be kissed chastely, she thought rebelliously; it was too late for that now, when her breasts were feeling tight and tingly and she was dying to slide her hands over his skin—all of which added to her inner turmoil and sense of injustice. 'I was wondering if you can turn this on and off like a tap—men can, can't they?' she said tartly.

He raised an eyebrow. 'That's a rather cynical remark. As a matter of fact there is a point of no return to which men are very vulnerable.'

Lucy said scathingly, 'I know that! It wasn't what I meant.'

'What did you mean?'

'I wondered why you—stopped. I mean to say,' she said, 'one minute you were kissing me, then you were laughing at me. It's not a very elevating experience, to be perfectly honest——'

'And probably entirely new to you? I'm so sorry,' he said seriously, 'but I wasn't actually laughing at *you*. Because as anyone with you in their arms would know——'

Lucy sat up abruptly. 'I hate the thought of that, Justin, so don't say another word!' she commanded.

He grimaced. 'It was meant as a compliment.'

'No, it was not! It was just like saying, give a man a girl who is reasonably attractive and—bingo. Which is something I resent very much.' Her eyes smouldered.

'Lucy,' he said thoughtfully, watching as she pulled her nightgown up, 'if you think it only takes a pretty girl who is eager——' their eyes clashed '—I grew out of that quite a few years back. Moreover, I was actually laughing at myself.'

She blinked. 'Why?'

'Because I was approaching that point of no return rather quickly,' he said with a faint, dry smile, twisting his lips.

'In spite of me trying to pretend I was too tired?'

'Are you?'

Lucy paused then said hollowly, 'I get the feeling I might never be.'

'Well, now,' he said gravely but with his grey eyes perfectly wicked, 'that's entirely appropriate for a wife.'

'But not essentially modest,' she whispered with a reluctant smile tugging at her lips.

'Wives are allowed to be sexy with their husbands. So long as it stops there.'

'But——'

'In fact so far as being a wife goes,' he overrode her, 'there's only one serious flaw I've found in you, Lucy.'

'I...' her lips dimpled at the corner '...talk too much?' she hazarded.

'Much too much. Will you come willingly and happily to bed with me now?'

She opened her mouth to say something along the lines of, Did he know why she'd been unwilling and unhappy earlier? But in the end she said simply, 'Yes, please.'

'Lucy—can't you drive any faster? The first yearling is due to go under the hammer in half an hour.'

'We won't be late, Sasha, trust me, but I don't want to get caught speeding,' Lucy said reasonably.

'I know, but all the same—I should have been there hours ago,' Sasha said fretfully. 'Not only for the horses but there's the hospitality tent to be set up and the Riverbend Saddlery display—why, oh, why did I have to break down in the middle of the most terrible peakhour traffic?'

'These things can't be helped,' Lucy said soothingly but with an unholy inner wriggle of amusement. For once in her life Sasha was looking less than her usual

soignée self. Her hair was ruffled, her face was hot, there
was a streak of grease down her beautiful tight-fitting
designer jeans, her handmade leather boots were scuffed
and her expression was strained. What had happened
was, when her car had broken down on the way to the
sales complex, she'd rung them from a phone booth and
Justin had said he'd go to the complex immediately and
that Lucy should bring Sasha once she'd extricated
herself from her difficulties. 'I'm sure Justin can cope,'
she added, and couldn't help the faintest tinge of irony
that accompanied her words.

'You don't like me, do you, Lucy?' Sasha replied as
she scrubbed the grease mark then cast an almost
vengeful look at Lucy's attire, which consisted of a
simple but striking coffee linen, A-line button-through
dress with a longish skirt, flat bronze suede shoes and
a marvellous straw hat with the brim upturned. Her hair
was loose beneath it and gleamed like silk, her skin was
clear, flawless and glowing, her lips were painted a
frosted bronzy pink and the lightest touch of Miss Dior
lay on the air as she moved.

Lucy couldn't help but be conscious of this scrutiny,
and she drew a deep breath and said as mildly as she
was able, 'You make it rather hard for me sometimes,
Sasha.'

'*You* . . .' But Sasha stopped, perhaps fortunately, and
went on in an entirely different strain as Lucy swore beneath her breath and slowed down and stopped as she
was flagged so to do by a policeman, 'You must have
been speeding after all!'

'I was about two kilometres over the speed limit,' Lucy
said tartly, 'And only because *you* were so—oh, well, if

this isn't a sucker spot, I've never seen one, anyway. Which I will tell him!'

Sasha groaned. 'We'll be later than ever! He's liable to throw you into gaol if you argue with him!'

'Argue with him?' Lucy smiled sweetly. 'I wouldn't dream of it—Officer,' she said to the large young policeman at her window, 'before you write a thing down on that ticket, may I say a few words in my defence? In fact, if you let me get out, I could say them even better!'

'Of all the...' Sasha appeared lost for words as they drove off, unticketed, several minutes later.

'What was wrong with it?' Lucy queried, grinning. 'I merely explained why we were in a bit of a rush, pointed out to him, quite deferentially I thought, that he really should be policing *dangerous* traffic situations and not sitting behind a bush picking off lone cars only exceeding the limit by a couple of kilometres, and I offered to donate the fine to his favourite charity if he would reconsider his position. Which he did.'

'Because he was drooling at the mouth,' Sasha said bitterly. 'But don't think Justin will be taken in by these schoolgirlish ways forever, Lucy. Oh, you may think you have him enslaved at the moment but it won't last. You're too young for him. And there's always Joanna... She did up the Sydney house, by the way; did you know it was all her doing? And I can't help wondering if Justin's flaunting you at her because he's still punishing her for marrying Tim Madden.'

Lucy clenched the steering-wheel until her knuckles went white but surprised herself as she said quite steadily, even gently, 'Sasha, I'll try to forget you ever said that to me. We're here,' she added flatly.

Try to forget, Lucy marvelled, as she sat in the stand reserved for vendors later and watched Sasha, none other, lead the Cawnpore filly into the ring to an excited buzz of the crowd.

Somehow or other Sasha had got rid of the grease stain, she saw, and was wearing a navy blazer with 'RIVERBEND' on the back, and she handled the filly lightly but expertly. And she was a magnificent filly, you couldn't deny it, with powerful quarters, a splendid deep chestnut coat with a small white blaze and one white foot, and an alert, intelligent eye as she surveyed the crowd with her ears pricked. And for a moment Lucy forgot all else as she watched.

Then Justin slid into the seat beside her and said wryly, 'She's handling it all like an old stager.'

'She's magnificent,' Lucy said with an odd lump in her throat.

'We could be in for a magnificent bidding duel too,' he said significantly as the auctioneer read through the filly's blood-lines. 'Apparently there's a South African syndicate here rather interested, as well as a sheikh from Saudi Arabia.'

'Oh! Where is he?'

'I doubt if he's here in person but that's his trainer over there.' He pointed.

'And the Maddens,' Lucy murmured. She'd spotted Joanna and Tim almost immediately—Joanna was dressed in eye-catching yellow that went superbly with her dark hair.

'Uh-huh. Here goes.'

But the bidding opened quietly and after a few minutes Lucy turned a concerned face to Justin—to see that he was quite relaxed. 'They're playing cat and mouse,' he said.

And indeed they were, because, as the tension mounted, the bids crept up then started to leap up and the buzz from the floor grew and flashbulbs popped while television crews crept among the crowd as they passed the quarter of a million mark, then you could have heard a pin drop as Tim Madden appeared to drop out and the South Africans competed with the Saudi sheikh's trainer until they too dropped off. And Lucy clutched Justin's hand, thinking it was over as the auctioneer called...*for the final and last time*! But before he could drop his hammer, Tim Madden's hand went up. There was pandemonium briefly then silence again, and finally a huge roar that sent the Cawnpore filly dancing across the ring with Sasha clinging grimly to her rearing bit, as she was knocked down to Tim Madden for a sales record.

And it was all recorded for posterity in the next day's newspapers as well as being on television that night—Lucy holding Justin's hand tightly and concentrating fiercely during the bidding, Justin hugging Lucy as the final hammer went down. Tim Madden, smiling quietly into his wife's eyes—both the Maddens and the Waites posing with the filly, Sasha posing with the filly—it went on for the rest of the day and half the night. People congratulating them, people interviewing them and in between the other five of the Riverbend consignment allotted to that day being sold most successfully to buyers who also wanted to be photographed with the breeders.

So that by the time they got home Lucy was genuinely exhausted. 'What a day!' she said as Justin closed the door behind them.

'I know—want anything?'

'Only bed.'

He picked her up, carried her upstairs and laid her down on the bed. 'You were wonderful.'

Lucy grimaced. 'I didn't do much! Cawnpore's daughter did it all.'

'I mean——' he started to unbutton her dress '—you were wonderful with the Press, with the proud new owners of six Riverbend progeny, everything a wife should be in those circumstances,' he said with a smile at the back of his eyes. 'A considerable asset.'

'I'm glad,' she said huskily. 'But you bred her, you saved her life when she got colic.'

'All in a day's work,' he said lightly. 'Sit up.'

Lucy did so obediently and he continued to undress her like a child, then slid her cream nightgown down her body. She suffered these ministrations gratefully then said thoughtfully, 'Justin?'

'Uh-huh?' He'd got up to change himself and looked over his shoulder at her.

'Tim Madden must have an *awful* lot of money.'

'He does.'

'More than the sheikh, do you think?'

'I doubt it—but enough. Why?'

'I just wondered.'

'Go to sleep, Lucy,' he said but gently, and sat down beside her again. 'No,' he put his fingers to her lips, 'not one more word—well, unless you'd like to explain to me why Sasha arrived today muttering about you corrupting the due processes of the law?'

Lucy sat up indignantly. 'Is that what she *said*? Why, if it hadn't been for her, I wouldn't have had to talk myself out of a speeding ticket in the first place. She really——'

'Talk yourself out of a speeding ticket, Lucy? I didn't think that was possible.'

'Well, it is. Provided you get them before they've written anything.'

He looked quizzically into her eyes. 'You've had a bit of experience in these things?'

'No, that's the first time—all it takes is a bit of eyelash-batting—oh, no,' she said on a descending scale. 'Justin, I wasn't being a *femme fatale* if that's what you're thinking, I never was, not really and anyway, there isn't a part of me now that's not wholly taken up with you and——' But she stopped abruptly and bit her lip.

'Then that's fine,' he said gravely. 'I approve whole-heartedly of what you just said. So don't look,' he said softly, 'as if you feel you ought to retract it. And now, my dear, it's definitely lights out and silence. But only if you'll let me get in with you and only if you'll allow me to hold you, because, as you once told me, that's very relaxing.'

Which was how Lucy came to fall asleep in his arms, still unable to deal with all the impressions of an exciting yet turbulent day—what Sasha had said, how Joanna had looked, how Tim and Justin had, for one brief but piercing moment before shaking hands, registered a cool yet battle-laden tension between them.

CHAPTER EIGHT

'Lucy, why don't you go home?' Justin said at about three o'clock the next afternoon. 'There's the Breeder's Ball tonight, don't forget, and you've been yawning for the past hour.'

'Sorry,' Lucy said, and promptly yawned again. 'OK.' She smiled up at him and he bent his head and kissed her lightly.

And once home, she changed, lay down on the settee to relax and bring her mind to bear on everything that had happened over the past few days, but fell asleep for a couple of hours. What is wrong with me—why am I so sleepy, why can't I come to grips with anything? she wondered as she woke up feeling terrible.

It proved nothing that a soak in the bath didn't cure, and she started to do her hair and her make-up but she was still conscious of a failing to come to grips with things. Perhaps, she lowered her brush, and stared at herself in the mirror, I shouldn't even try. What can I do to change things, anyway? How can I alter that deep hostility between Justin and Tim Madden? How can I help Joanna, and so far as Sasha's concerned, I can only hope to God she's wrong and perhaps it's about time I was a bit more charitable...

'Lucy?'

Her eyes widened as she registered Justin's image in the mirror. 'I didn't hear you come home!'

'I know, you were miles away,' he said wryly. 'What I'm wondering is, where?'

'So *much* has happened lately,' she said hastily. 'It must be that. I slept for a couple of hours and woke up feeling like a log of wood!'

'You don't look anything like a log of wood at the moment.' His grey gaze drifted down her.

She smoothed her towelling robe, took an inward breath and turned to him with a mischievous little glint in her eye as she said softly, 'You ain't seen nothin' yet, brother!'

He laughed and looked rueful at the same time. 'I only hope I can bear it.'

Her ballgown was rather modest in design, a long flowing skirt with a matching sleeveless gilet that buttoned to the throat and came to her knees. What made it quite stunning, however, was that the lined silk chiffon it was created from matched the deep pansy-blue of her eyes and the buttons down the front of the gilet were beautiful little prancing pearl, amethyst and diamante horses...

'There,' she said, standing before Justin at last. She'd put her hair up again, and dotted in it were tiny flowers fashioned from the same silk chiffon as the outfit. Her purse and shoes were silver.

He started to smile as he surveyed her. 'Where did you find it?'

Her mouth dimpled at the corners. 'I've got the feeling it found me. As soon as I saw it, I thought, now how could I wear anything else to a Breeder's Ball!'

'How indeed.'

'It's also very comfortable.' She twirled before him to demonstrate. 'Very suitable for dancing, and I know there'll be nobody in another one because it's unique and—cost an awful lot of your money, Justin.' She came to rest in front of him again and put a hand to her mouth just a little awkwardly. 'Not that these are real——' she touched a button '—but I hope you don't mind.'

'Why should I mind?' he queried.

'Well, even my father,' she said soberly, 'used to get a bit shocked about the price of these kinds of clothes. Oh, dear, I'm beginning to wish I'd never said those words about being a careful, prudent wife. I've got the feeling they're going to haunt me.'

'Lucy——' he touched the point of her chin '—I, on the other hand, am quite happy to fork out a small fortune to see you looking so happy and stunning. Just remember that.'

'That's...lovely,' she said with an odd attack of shyness, 'but it won't take that, I promise. You know,' she went on before he could reply, 'you look rather devastating yourself.' And indeed he did in a black dinner suit, pleated white shirt and hand-tied bow-tie. 'I might have to keep a sharp eye out for any ladies on the loose!'

In the car, she said suddenly, 'I suppose they'll all be there.'

'I guess so.'

They were.

The Maddens, Sasha although with an escort, a tall, good-looking man, the South Africans, the sheikh's trainer—and courtesy of the Breeder's Association they were all at the same table...

I can handle this, Lucy told herself after taking a deep breath, and went forward with her head tilted regally.

It was Sasha she had to handle first, Sasha who came to sit next to her after dinner had been cleared and a general loosening up of the company occurred as the band struck up.

Sasha said stiffly as she slipped into a vacant chair next to Lucy, 'I would like to apologise.'

Surprise made Lucy's eyes widen as she surveyed the other girl, who was wearing a black strapless gown and a troubled expression in her green eyes. 'Well, thank you,' she said slowly. 'Perhaps I've been—a bit at fault too.'

But Sasha brushed that aside. 'I should never have said what I did. It was only... sheer jealousy that made me do it. You see, after he broke up with Joanna, who incidentally is a friend of mine, I,' Sasha stopped and looked unbelievably uncomfortable. 'Well, I thought there might be some hope for me—only to have that idea crushed by a slip of a girl—by you, I mean, and it... rather brought out the worst in me, I'm afraid.'

Lucy blinked and sought a little frantically for the means to cope with this. 'Uh...I, well I wondered about that; I mean to say——'

'You don't have to say anything, Lucy,' Sasha said drily. 'I was never a contender; I just couldn't bring myself to believe it.'

'What did...I mean, why now?' Lucy asked involuntarily.

Sasha looked away, looked oddly flustered then her eyes came to rest on her escort and she said perfunctorily, 'I've met someone else.'

Lucy stared at her averted profile and wondered why this didn't ring true.

Then Sasha spoke again, 'I'm leaving Justin, by the way.'

Lucy sat up. 'Oh, dear! Do you have to? I mean, I——'

'Yes, I have to, Lucy—I should have done it years ago. I'll tell him tonight.' She looked up as a shadow fell across them but it was Joanna Madden and she said gaily. 'May I join you? All the men of the party are talking bloodlines!' She grimaced expressively. 'So I swapped my seat with one of them.'

'Of course,' both Lucy and Sasha said, but perhaps for the only time in their acquaintance they were united in the oddly very brief but wary glance they exchanged as Joanna sat down. And Lucy, looking across the table, discovered Justin watching them before he switched his grey eyes away as someone spoke to him. How strange, she thought. Three women either in love with him or having loved him. What is he thinking? What is everyone else thinking? Probably, she thought with an inner tremor, they're wondering how Lucy Waite will cope with an old mistress and a would-be mistress, so I'll just have to show them...

'Have you thought of a name for the Cawnpore filly yet, Joanna?' she said brightly.

'I've thought of sixty,' Joanna replied whimsically, 'but none of them is quite right. Did you have any thoughts on the subject, Lucy? Or Sasha?'

'Well, I always give them pet names,' Sasha said wryly. 'I used to call her Flopsy because as a baby she used to flop all over the place, but I did think of—well, he *did* save her life and I wondered about—Justine.'

Sasha, Lucy thought. How could you put your foot in it like that? As if Tim Madden is going to have any horse named after someone who lived with and loved his wife...

But Joanna handled it superbly. She said, 'Tell me how he saved her life!'

And Sasha launched into graphic account of the colic and how Justin had kept the filly on her feet and walked and walked her, how he was the only one she trusted enough to help her through her pain and misery.

'Were you there too, Lucy?' Joanna said in a bid, probably, to stem the tide.

'Well, no; Lucy,' Sasha said, 'chose to get herself lost that day——'

'It was the next day, actually,' Lucy inserted gently, 'and I didn't choose to do it, it happened quite out of the blue—oh!' She looked up as she felt a hand on her shoulder and was intensely grateful to see it was Justin.

'May I have this dance, Lucy?'

'I'd be *delighted*,' she said and stood up with a flourish, adding under her breath, 'I really need to get away!'

But it wasn't until they'd joined the growing throng on the floor and he took her in his arms that he said with a smile lurking in his eyes but also something rather querying, 'Care to tell me why you needed rescuing so urgently?'

'Well, to be quite candid,' she replied, 'I was about to... It was Sasha,' she said ruefully. 'She has about as much tact as a tank!'

'What's she said now?'

Did that odd question mark in his eyes subside, she wondered then suddenly remembered Sasha's apology and the fact that she was leaving Justin. 'Oh, it was nothing,' she said.

'Lucy——'

'No, Justin, I'd rather not be trite and petty,' she said determinedly, then grinned up at him. 'Have you any idea how good a dancer I am?'

'You could always show me.'

She did, and she really let her hair down and soon the whole party caught her enthusiasm.

But what came as stunning little surprise to someone who could and had quite frequently danced the night away was how, just before midnight, she suddenly discovered she didn't want to be doing it any more and there was only one thing she did want to be doing but Justin was dancing with someone else, and she could only sit and stare helplessly at him as she thought of the way he made love to her or just held her in his arms when they went to bed.

And when he came back she responded mechanically to the conversation for a little while until he frowned slightly and stood up and made their farewells.

Of course there were the usual friendly remarks passed about 'the night being young but then so was their marriage', and more friendly raillery, when Lucy suddenly blushed brightly.

They didn't speak until they were home.

Then he led her into the bedroom and turned her to face him in the middle of the floor.

'Lucy?'

She winced.

He put a finger beneath her chin and made her look up. 'What's wrong?'

'Nothing...'

He raised his other hand and started to undo the little prancing horses. 'You could have fooled me.' He slid the gilet off.

'I just—didn't want to be there any more.'

'That was increasingly obvious.'

She grimaced, wondering if she'd caused another set of people to wonder seriously about her.

'On the other hand, if you wanted to be here, like this——' he reached for the zip of her skirt and it slipped to the floor '—there's nothing wrong in that.'

'You knew,' she accused, blushing again, and her body trembled.

His gaze was slightly amused as it roamed over her, wearing nothing now but a bra, a lacy suspender belt and equally lacy undies and sheer nylons, all blue, as she stepped over her skirt.

'I suspected,' he murmured.

'So did everyone else,' she said rather wretchedly and put her hands to her cheeks. 'How embarrassing.'

'There still nothing wrong in it. In fact, I'll go further.' He released her bra and drew it off her breasts. 'Don't change.'

'But I'll have to—I can't go around being so transparent!'

He laughed softly and put his hands round her waist. 'So long as I don't mind, that's all there is to worry about, my beautiful ch...' He stopped.

'Child?' she whispered. 'You must really think I am one now.'

He stared down at her naked breasts and the lovely curve of her hips, the delicate satiny softness of her skin. 'No, you're not, Lucy,' he said at last, 'and don't let me ever make you feel like one; you're just...you. Rather perfect, in fact.'

She wanted to ask him if he just meant her body or if it was the kind of perfection he could love, really love, as he'd loved Joanna. She desperately, she suddenly realised, wanted to ask him to be honest about Joanna Madden and ask him why he was subjecting her to this close contact, although, she supposed, the alternative would have been to leave her at Dalkeith and realistically she couldn't expect to avoid them forever. But something held her back, she couldn't really say what, other than the feeling that the ball was in her court now—she loved him, she was married to him and it was up to her to make the best of it, in other words. And at least one problem had resolved itself—Sasha. And yet, had it? Why was there this question mark in her mind about Sasha?

She sighed inwardly but said in a deep, husky little voice, 'Well, so are you.'

He smiled absently. 'No. Far from it, unfortunately, but——'

'Justin——' she reached out and placed her fingertips to his lips '—do you know why else I wanted to get away?'

'No.'

'I—seriously want to be alone with you for a while. Just us. We only seem to be together in a passing sort of way, don't we?'

'We don't exactly do this in passing, though. But I know what you mean—Lucy, I'm sorry about all this,' he said abruptly. 'And that includes Sasha, Joanna——'

'Did Sasha tell you?' Lucy asked, her eyes widening. 'Yes——'

'*I'm* sorry about that. I didn't—it really wasn't anything I did.' She hesitated, then added honestly, 'Other than being married to you.'

'I know.' He smiled, but it didn't reach his eyes and he moved his hands on her waist then pulled her into his arms. '*I* really didn't mean for it to be such a traumatic experience, marriage to me. And unfortunately, with Sasha leaving like this, I won't be able to do anything about the Seychelles for a little while, but as *soon* as possible, we will. In the meantime, though, at least we'll be at home alone together. How about that?'

She didn't have to tell him what she thought. It must have shown in her eyes.

But first thing in the morning came the news via the newspaper that Tim Madden had suffered a massive heart attack at the Breeder's Ball and was critically ill.

'Justin!' Lucy whispered, her face paling. They were in bed together and he'd made some tea and brought the paper up without unrolling it. And for a long moment they simply stared at the newsprint picture—the one of themselves and the Maddens with the Cawnpore filly. 'It must have happened after we left.'

Justin lifted his face and in spite of herself Lucy was shocked at the deep lines of tension scored into it. But before she could say any more the phone rang—it was Sasha, but it was difficult from his monosyllable replies to make much sense of it. And when he put the phone down he got out of bed immediately and started to pull some clothes on almost at random—jeans and a black T-shirt.

'What did she say?' Lucy asked.

He came to sit beside her and took her hands in his. 'She was there when it happened, Lucy. Apparently he's had a history of heart disease although very few people knew about it. Joanna is devastated and has no one to turn to. His family always resented him marrying

someone so much younger, and she has no family of her
own. Sasha has been with her all night but there's quite
a bit of unpleasantness floating around. One of his sons
actually accused Joanna of driving him to an early grave
and tried to keep her from his bedside. He also made
the accusation that spending so much money on the
Cawnpore filly as a thrust in his private duel with me
over her, was the *coup de grâce*. Lucy...'

'You have to go to her,' she whispered.

'Will you come with me?'

'I...no, Justin. Not this time.'

'Lucy——' He broke off and looked tortured for a
moment. Then he said very quietly, 'It's *over* between
us, just remember that.'

'I will, I promise,' she whispered. And he kissed her
and held her hard. He also said, 'I love you, Lucy Waite.'
And was gone.

She lay back and thought that it was probably true,
in a way. She also lay and wondered what good his
presence in the midst of the Madden family crisis would
do. And she couldn't stop herself from wondering what
would happen if Tim Madden died...

That day was the longest of Lucy's life as Tim Madden's
life hung in the balance. Justin rang a couple of times
but in between those times all she could do was think.
And find herself going over everything in her mind,
round and round in circles, and coming up with some
surprises... Sasha, for example, who she had not known
was an old friend of Joanna's and who had proved to
be a good enough friend to support her during the awful
night that had just passed. Sasha, who had admitted it
was only after Joanna and Justin had broken up that

she'd allowed herself to hope there could be a place for *her* in Justin's life. Sasha, Lucy thought, who so suddenly and surprisingly ended her little war with me but couldn't truthfully tell me why. Because she knows now, if she ever doubted it, that it's *still* Joanna she would have to fight for Justin in his heart if nothing else, not me?

She was sitting in the lounge staring into space when Justin came home. It was a dark overcast afternoon and she wore jeans and a long-sleeved cream silk blouse with her hair tied back in a blue ribbon. And her eyes were shadowed and wary as she stood up slowly when the door opened.

He came wearily into the lounge and she was shocked again to see the lines of tension in his face. Nor could she find any way to frame the query that was uppermost in her mind.

And his grey eyes ranged over, standing so still before he said quietly, 'He's going to be all right. The crisis is past but it will be a long, slow recovery.'

'Oh, thank God,' Lucy whispered, and sank down as her legs seemed to fold up beneath her.

He came to sit beside her on the settee, took her hand laid his head back wearily. And they simply sat like that for some minutes in silence. Until Lucy made herself say, 'How is Joanna?'

'All right now.'

'And the...his family?'

He sat up and pressed her hand before releasing it. 'They've come back to earth a bit; a lot of what was said was said under awful pressure.' He rubbed the blue shadows on his jaw wearily. 'Lucy——'

'Justin,' she said before he could go on and because she couldn't help herself, 'didn't they think it strange you should be there?'

He grimaced. 'It didn't exactly help at first, but I think I made them realise I was only there as an—intermediary. Joanna, you see——'

But Lucy stood up suddenly. 'You must be—would you like something to eat? You probably haven't had anything all day. I'll make us something now. How about a drink in the meantime? Stay there, I'll get it,' she said brightly, but to herself she was saying, I'm sorry, I know I brought it up but I can't talk about Joanna Madden any more, Justin, I just can't!

'Lucy——' He stood up, caught her wrist and for a moment towered over her, dark and powerful, and she trembled inwardly but didn't know that she looked both frightened and rebellious.

'Don't,' she stammered, not quite sure what she meant but suddenly sure it was all too much for her.

He paused, his eyes narrowed. 'Don't what, Lucy?' he said evenly after a long moment.

'I...I—let's just leave it, please, Justin.' Her voice shook but there was the sudden light of determination in her eyes. 'Let's just...pretend it's all over.'

'Lucy, it *is*, and——'

'Well, good! Now if you'll let me go I'll get us something to eat—really, Justin,' she tried to laugh, 'you're hurting me.'

He released her wrist abruptly then picked it up again and inspected the white marks of his fingers on it. Then he looked into her eyes and said drily, 'I'm only trying to reassure you, Lucy——'

'Oh, I'm reassured,' she broke in again. 'Is there any hope that we could go home now, by the way, Justin?'

He said after a tense moment, 'Tomorrow morning if you like—Lucy, will you come to Riverbend with me for a while?'

Her eyes widened. 'Why?'

'Because that's where I'll have to be for most of the time until I find a replacement for Sasha.'

'Well...' She hesitated, because in her heart she was dying to get back to Dalkeith.

'We could bring Shirley and Adrian from Dalkeith.'

'All right,' she said slowly.

'After all, it is your second home now and,' he grimaced, 'it certainly needs someone to take an interest in it.'

But although that was what they did, things were different.

CHAPTER NINE

I KNEW this wasn't a good idea, coming to Riverbend, Lucy thought a week later. Which was not to say there was anything lacking at Riverbend other than a little tender loving care, which Shirley was more than happy to provide. It was a more modern house than Dalkeith but still a pleasant, gracious home. But its relative unfamiliarity was unsettling in her mood of the moment, which alternated between a kind of numbness and a kind of grief that contrived to make her stiff and awkward with Justin, withdrawn and then trying too hard and altogether right off balance.

She would also look around the rooms at times, and wonder if Joanna had designed them... There are no ghosts at Dalkeith, she thought more than once, that's why I'd be better off there. But, there was no doubt Justin couldn't have been at Dalkeith at this time; it was the peak of the foaling season and without Sasha there was undoubtedly a mountain of work entailed in running the stud, not to mention the personal interest Justin took in the horses.

For not only did Riverbend run its own mares but it stood four stallions, each of which had a list of outside mares booked to it, and nearly all of these mares arrived to be served with a foal at foot and they had to be accommodated in pastures, they had to be served and kept on the property until they tested positive to the service and their foals had to be looked after as well.

She said once to Justin, 'It's like a production line! No sooner have they dropped their foals than they're put *in* foal again; it doesn't seem terribly fair to me.'

'But it can't be news to you either, Lucy,' he replied with a faint look of amusement.

'Well, no, it's not,' she confessed, 'but on *this* scale...I mean, we're all but swamped with mares and foals and...' She gestured helplessly. 'It's a logistical nightmare if nothing else.'

'I can only agree, at times,' he commented wryly. 'That's why Sasha was so good; she had the kind of brain and horse-sense that excelled in these circumstances.'

'Have you...have you heard what she's doing now?'

'Yes I have. She's got a job with the Magic Millions organisation.'

'Oh! You mean the Queensland sales where all the yearlings sold are eligible for the Magic Millions race?'

'None other. It should suit her eminently.'

'How are you going finding a replacement for her?' Lucy asked after a moment.

'I've had a flood of applicants. It will take a bit of whittling down.'

'Could I help in the meantime?' Lucy said suddenly. 'I...I need something to do.'

They were breakfasting together but Justin had been up all night with a foal that had got entangled in a fence. The fact of this, that they had so little time to spend together, was something Lucy didn't know whether she was glad about or not. Because, in truth, whatever had snapped within her that last afternoon in Sydney had stayed snapped, and she knew she was subtly holding Justin at arm's length, knew he knew, but perhaps the most heartbreaking aspect of it all was that he'd made no real effort to break down her defences.

Well, look, he's been incredibly busy and I can understand why, she told herself a little drearily several times. All the same...

Which was not to say she hadn't shared his bed since that day, nor that he hadn't made love to her. But what she couldn't say in all honesty was that the thought that they might be interrupted by an emergency call from the stables, as did happen once when a very valuable mare got into difficulties foaling late one evening, was the real reason for her subdued, slightly tense response, although she'd offered it when she'd sensed he was about to say something. Offered it with a strained little smile then tried, too hard, to be bright and perky while she was feeling like dying within, and more so when he'd let it go...

'If you want to, Lucy,' he said at last, his grey eyes lingering on her.

'Yes, I do.' She realised immediately that she sounded defiant and stubborn, for no good reason probably, was cross with herself then tossed her head in a further gesture of defiance.

He said nothing as their gazes caught and clashed. Then, with an oddly dry inflection, he said abruptly, 'What's wrong, Lucy?'

'Nothing. Nothing in the world!' she answered brightly, and forced the tears that were so close to stay away. 'Where shall I start and what shall I do?'

She held her breath as she thought he was going to contest her statement, but although his mouth set in a rather hard line, he said unemotionally, 'There is something you could do. When the outside mares are delivered or picked up by their owners, it would be handy to have someone in the stud office who could give them a bit of a tour of the place, spend a bit of time with them—that kind of thing. It makes them feel wanted.'

Lucy's eyes widened with genuine interest. 'I think I'd like that,' she said slowly.

'I think you'd probably be good at it,' he commented.

'That would be a change,' she murmured, and bit her lip.

'Lucy——'

'No, Justin,' she sprang up and managed to grin at him, 'don't take any notice of me. I *do* know I'm very good at talking the hind leg off a donkey! Can I start today?'

'By all means,' he said, but after another lingering, narrowed look. Then he shrugged and stood up himself. 'I'm going to grab a few hours' sleep. I don't suppose you'd care to—join me?'

Her lips parted, her eyes widened and her heart started to beat erratically. But she said, 'I've not been...up that long, Justin. I mean...' She trailed off awkwardly.

He looked down at her enigmatically for an age then he touched the point of her chin gently and said, 'I know what you mean, Lucy. Never mind. Why don't you wander off to the stud office and—get started?' But there was a look of irony in his grey eyes that pierced her heart.

She hesitated then turned and walked away, her emotions in turmoil. What does he expect? she asked herself miserably. Surely he must *know* I can't help wondering what would have happened if Tim Madden had died, that I just can't stop thinking about it as well as everything else...

* * *

And for the next few weeks she threw herself into her newly created job as the flow of mares went both ways, incoming and outgoing. She also unexpectedly met an old friend, a young man who'd just qualified as a vet and was assisting their regular vet. He was a couple of years older but he'd been born in the district and they'd moved in the same crowd after she'd left school but only as friends. He was apparently delighted to meet her again and they had a few chats, recalling old times and laughing a lot. He was a tall, well-built, open-faced young man with a shock of blond curly hair and with one serious passion in his life, horses—Lucy gathered he had no romantic attachment at the moment. But in the uncomplicated pleasure she found in his company, she failed to notice that he looked at her occasionally with new eyes. It didn't occur to her for two reasons: because she wasn't looking for it and because she didn't imagine, now she was a married woman, that men would seriously think of her in those terms.

Nor would she ever have been aware of it if she hadn't one day been laughing over her shoulder at something he said as she walked past then looked ahead to see Justin watching them, standing curiously still.

She took an unexpected breath as she walked towards him, her eyes widening as he still made no move, but his grey gaze seemed to pierce hers for a blinding moment. Then at last he moved and said with a wry twist of his lips, 'Hi, Lucy. Having fun?'

'Yes—no, I mean...Justin?' She frowned at him. 'Is something wrong?'

'No, of course not, Lucy,' he said easily. But it was that evening he told her that he had to go to Sydney for several days...

*　　*　　*

'Lucy?'

'Oh! Justin.' She looked up with a smile from the brown study she'd been in since returning from the stables. 'I didn't hear you come in. Finished for the day?'

'Yes.' He threw down his hat and stretched. 'You're looking very pensive,' he remarked.

'I was feeling a bit pensive,' she confessed but added as she stood up, 'Dinner is actually ready but I'll tell Shirley to hold it for half an hour so you can have a shower. Would you like a drink?'

For a moment, his grey gaze roamed over her narrowly and she thought he was going to ask her what she'd been pensive about, but then a faint smile touched his lips and he turned away saying, 'I'd love one. I'll be back in ten minutes.'

And they had their dinner then took their coffee on to the terrace where a crescent moon laid a silvery glow over the landscape.

'Summer's really here,' Lucy murmured, and once again he let his gaze drift over her, taking in her sleeveless white blouse and white cotton skirt splashed with yellow daisies.

'Mmm. It will be Christmas before we know where we are. Lucy, now that things have calmed down a bit, I have to go away for a few days—a week at the most. Sydney mainly, and all business. I've narrowed the applicants for Sasha's job down to two and I'll be seeing them but if you'd like to come——'

'No, thank you,' she said hastily, then forced herself to relax. 'There are still a few mares coming and going. I can keep on with my job here if you like.'

'It's what *you* would like,' he said, and there was something curiously watchful and narrowed in his eyes.

She frowned faintly. 'I know you keep asking me this but it seems to be my turn now—is something wrong? I've——' she paused '—known Rob Redding for years and years, if that...' She stopped and stared at him.

But he only, once again, said wryly, 'So have I. It makes me feel quite old. Good to see him qualified. I think he'll make a top vet from what I've seen so far. No, nothing's wrong, Lucy—as you keep telling me.'

She sat back and grimaced. 'I wondered if you thought I was being a *femme fatale* again.'

'No.' He was silent for a long while then he stretched and yawned. 'I don't know about you but I'm knackered, and I've got a crack-of-dawn start tomorrow.'

'Oh,' Lucy said with some concern. 'I promised Adrian I'd help him with a composition he's got to have in for the School of the Air tomorrow. He has to read it out over the radio.'

'Never mind,' Justin said, curiously gently, as he stood up. Then he bent over and kissed her briefly on the forehead. 'Goodnight, my dear. I'll try not to wake you in the morning and I'll ring you from Sydney.'

'Goodnight,' Lucy said in a strange little voice, and watched him walk away unhurriedly with a stabbing sense of grief in her heart.

It didn't go away over the next couple of days, that sense of grief, nor did her job, or Rob Redding, or even Adrian's getting an A for his composition mitigate it. All she could think of was lying stiff and silent beside Justin that night when she did go to bed, longing for him to wake up and take her in his arms, willing herself to reach out and touch him but not being able to do it as she wondered whether he would be seeing Joanna in Sydney...

Then came the proof that he had in the form of a picture in a two-day-old newspaper she normally wouldn't have bothered reading if Shirley, who was still avid for her hometown news however late it might be, hadn't left it on the kitchen table.

She stared down at it and drew in a long, shaky breath. Ever since they'd left Sydney, she realised, she'd longed to ask Justin for news of the Maddens, but it had seemed like tempting fate as well as establishing whether he'd been in touch—if he had, would she mind? And yet it was not unreasonable for him to do so, but... Well, he has now, she thought unhappily, and wiped away a foolish tear. For the picture that had captured her attention was one of Justin and Joanna, with his hand on her elbow, leaving the Sydney hospital where Tim Madden was still recovering, and it was dated the day after he had arrived back in Sydney two days ago. It also bore a simple but cryptic caption to the effect that the Waite-Madden feud appeared to have been halted in its tracks.

Why didn't he tell me? she wondered miserably. That it wasn't *all* business.

To make matters worse, she was out riding when he rang that day—he'd rung daily—so what she got was a message that he'd call early the next morning, and would she please make sure she was in the house? To explain? she wondered dully. He's left it a bit late, or perhaps he thinks the odds against my seeing it are pretty long. And why doesn't he ring back this evening when I'm *sure* to be here? Is he with...her? I don't know how much longer I can stand this uncertainty and torment.

And the next morning Justin explained nothing, nor did he mention the Maddens, but he did say he would be home the following day late in the afternoon, that he'd appointed Sasha's replacement, and asked her how she was.

'Fine. Fine!' she reassured him.

'Good. No other problems?'

'Not that I know of!'

'OK—see you tomorrow, Lucy.' And he rang off.

It was a moment before she put the phone down, and she said to it before she did so, I'm not terribly sure about that, Justin. Because, you see, I just don't think I can go on living with the thought of you and Joanna...any longer.

And two days later she sat in Mother Angelica's study at her old school, a room she was very familiar with and which was quite unchanged since she'd first come to know it at nine, and said jerkily, 'I need some advice— thank you for seeing me at such short notice, by the way, but I'm afraid I've got myself into a bit of a bind.'

Mother Angelica's hair was grey now beneath the short veil and there were new lines and wrinkles in her skin, but her tall, spare figure was the same and her keen blue eyes especially were as uncomfortably all-seeing as they'd ever been. 'So it would appear, Lucy,' she said thought-fully. 'And talking of by-the-ways, I would have liked to know about your marriage at least; it would have been a courtesy if nothing else.'

Lucy sighed. 'No, it wouldn't. Because, you see, I married my worst enemy—or so I thought at the time. I married for all the wrong reasons, not to say *crazy* reasons only—then I fell in love with him and realised

I'd probably *always* been a little in love with him but he loves someone else, someone he can't have, except that her husband nearly died a few weeks ago and if he had... well, I just can't stop thinking about it. You see, *if* he had, they could have been together again—if it weren't for me.'

'My dear child——' Mother Angelica began, but Lucy interrupted her.

'I'm *not* a child any more,' she said intensely, her eyes suddenly flashing blue fire in her white, weary face. 'That's how *he* thinks of me but I'm a living, breathing woman now. In all respects save one: I haven't had a child myself yet.'

'And you think that's what it takes?' Mother Angelica said quietly.

Lucy stared at her. 'What do you mean?' she said hollowly after a moment.

'Well, neither have I. But it's to me you've brought your problems, Lucy.'

Lucy grimaced. 'That's because you more or less brought me up, thankless task though it may have been, but——'

'On the contrary, Lucy. I always felt I was working with the finest material.'

'*What*?' Lucy whispered, her eyes now astounded.

'But what was more,' the nun went on in that same thoughtful, quiet way, 'despite our frequent conflicts, I always hoped that you acquired enough respect for me to benefit from my upbringing—however old-fashioned it may have seemed at the time.'

Lucy blinked several times then said hoarsely, 'Yes, I did. And yes, that's why I'm here, but——'

'Very well. Let's take this step by step, my dear—and I apologise for calling you a child.'

So that was what they did. And at the end Mother Angelica sat silent for a time then she said, 'I'm surprised at you, Lucy. I thought you had more spirit.'

Which was not what Lucy was expecting, and her eyes widened. 'Do you mean . . . ?'

'I mean, if you really love this man, why aren't you fighting for him?'

Lucy actually laughed, although it was a pale imitation. 'You know,' she said, 'I came here all prepared for you to talk about the sanctity of marriage, but not this.'

'It's not a lot different,' Mother Angelica commented.

Lucy was silent for a moment, then she said painfully, 'But he does make me feel like a child sometimes and there are . . .' She stopped, then said awkwardly, 'And there are things between men and, well, women that are hard to explain——'

'Especially to a woman who has no experience of men in that way? I believe you,' Mother Angelica said, 'but I don't believe it should change one's morals or the things *you* believe in or be a cause to run away—does he know where you are?'

'No,' Lucy said distractedly. 'What did you mean about the things *I* believe in?'

'That you're a woman not a child, that you love him, have given yourself to him and are entitled to do all those things. But I wouldn't be saying this, Lucy,' Mother Angelica narrowed her eyes, 'if it didn't seem to me that you also respect him. Or if I felt he was some sort of bounder who had taken terrible advantage of a rather innocent young woman—which is how it would appear to a lot of people on the face of things.'

'I know, but that's not quite... It wasn't quite like that. As a matter of fact, I respect him as much as I do you,' Lucy said shakenly.

'Then you've forgiven him for marrying you the way he did?' There was an even more acute than normal little glint in those blue eyes now.

Lucy paused. 'I did have another option; I couldn't bring myself to take it, as I told you,' she said at last. 'What I didn't realise at the time was how difficult it would be to live with the thought of him loving someone else.'

'You haven't done it for very long.'

'No.'

'And apart from this feeling that he doesn't love you the way you love him, how has he treated you?'

'Very well—look, I'm not denying that he might love me in a way,' Lucy said desperately. 'Or that he would ever stop taking care of me and all that. I don't even think he would dishonour me intentionally, although...' She stopped. 'It's just this awful feeling that I'm not his...soulmate, and she is.'

'Why don't you give him the benefit of the doubt? Men,' Mother Angelica said, 'can change their minds. We all can.'

Lucy sat in confused silence for about two minutes, then she said, 'Could I stay here just for a while?'

'Of course, but I do think you should get in touch with him in a day or two if you've run away and he doesn't know where you are.'

'You do?'

'Wouldn't it feel cowardly to hide away from him for any longer?'

'Well I suppose so...'

In the event she wasn't given the opportunity to do so for any longer by Justin either, but it was quite by accident that she overheard what he and Mother Angelica had to say to each other when Justin arrived at the convent to look for her quite early the next morning. She *had* been with the junior boarders playing an early game of rounders; that was where Mother had left her when she was called away, following her obvious intention of not allowing Lucy to mope or brood in the plain, rather cell-like guest-room. The previous afternoon Lucy had been called upon to umpire a couple of tennis matches and in the evening she'd been roped in to play the piano at an end-of-year concert rehearsal, then have a late supper with that year's senior girls.

But in the middle of the rounders she'd been struck by a mixture of regret that things were no longer so simple for her and the urgent thought that she had to sit down somewhere peaceful and private and *think*. She chose the little walled garden that was off limits to the girls and thus was new to her, without stopping to think that it was also directly below Mother Angelica's first floor study.

There was a bench, a patch of lawn, a bird bath, creepers along the grey stone walls and a riot of roses. There was also, as she sat down and leant back in the early sunlight and closed her eyes, the sound of voices suddenly from above, quite distinct and very familiar...

'How do you do, Mother Angelica? I'm Justin Waite and I've come to enquire whether you've seen or heard anything about my wife who would have been known to you as Lucy Wainright of Dalkeith.'

Lucy swallowed and sat upright abruptly.

'Ah, Mr Waite! I have as a matter of fact been looking forward to having a few words with you. Please sit down.' There was a slight pause and the sound of a chair on wood. 'Now,' Mother Angelica continued in a voice Lucy recognised only too well, and her eyes widened, 'would you please be so good as to tell me *why* you took a girl as naïve and vulnerable as Lucy and forced her into a marriage of convenience? I can think of a very unpleasant name for the likes of you, you know.'

Lucy gasped.

'Is that what she told you, Mother Angelica?' There was the faintest suggestion of a drawl in Justin's voice, but it was mainly as hard and cold as the nun's.

'No, it is not what she told me. She apparently admires and respects you and indeed, thinks she *loves* you. So much so that she is prepared to leave you so that you and some other woman can be together again and be— soulmates,' Mother Angelica said with utter, icy contempt, then, 'I'm waiting, Mr Waite.'

'Madam,' Justin said softly but equally as icily, 'I have no intention of being soulmates with anyone other than Lucy, so——'

'Then how come she's not aware of this?' Mother Angelica broke in imperiously. 'How come this lovely child who was so radiant, so spirited even when she was so lonely at times, who made it a better day in most people's life even when she was being wayward, a child who is nevertheless completely *wholesome*—is like a broken flower now? Tell me that, Mr Waite?'

Lucy dropped her head into her hands and could have died.

'Look, Mother Angelica, just tell me where she is,' Justin said harshly. 'It may come as some surprise to you but I care as much about Lucy and her welfare as you do.'

'Then you have a strange way of showing it, Mr Waite.'

'Would you rather I'd abandoned her after her father died, ma'am?'

There was a little pause and the tension of it seemed to float down to where Lucy sat so that she raised her head—and waited.

'Why did you marry her, then—will you tell me that?' Mother Angelica said in a very slightly, less hostile voice.

'I'll tell you this—I have no thought of *corrupting* her if that's what you fear; I have only her best interests at heart. I too, you see,' he said with considerable irony, 'was aware from the start of not only her innocence but her vulnerability when her father died, her loneliness, the terrible burden of debt and so on she'd been left with. And if I may bring this to your notice, Mother Angelica, I've known her for even longer than you have, so I too know all about the quite—special person Lucy Wainright is.'

'Will you at least admit you haven't been able to make her happy, Mr Waite?'

Lucy twisted her hands until her fingers went white.

'So it would seem so far,' Justin said drily. 'That doesn't mean to say I'll stop trying. Is she still here?'

A pause then Mother Angelica said, 'Yes,' and went on in a different, thoughtful voice, 'If I've misjudged you in some ways, Mr Waite, I apologise. But I still must admonish you to banish all thoughts of this other woman from your mind, because I hold you entirely responsible for Lucy—do I make myself clear?'

'Eminently, Mother Angelica. It so happens I hold *myself* entirely responsible for her, so we are—in some agreement...'

Lucy heard no more, because she sprang up suddenly and ran to her room, where she started to pack hastily. But she wasn't quick enough, because there was a brief knock on the door—and Mother Angelica opened it with Justin just behind her.

'Lucy...what are you doing?'

Lucy cast one look at Justin from beneath her lashes and was shocked to see how pale and tired he looked before she rushed into speech. 'Packing. Hello, Justin. I...I didn't expect to see you. Oh what's the use?' she said under her breath and sank down on to the bed, 'Look, quite by accident I happened to overhear your conversation so I have to say some things—thank you for defending me the way you did, Mother, but I'm not quite such a broken flower as you imagine and——'

'*Lucy!*'

'It wasn't my fault, I just happened to be sitting in the garden below your window; I wanted to be somewhere quiet where I could think,' Lucy said tiredly, and turned to look at Justin properly for the first time. 'And thank you for feeling so responsible for me, but I probably know better than most how...impossible it is to banish someone from your thoughts unless there's no hope, and even then perhaps, so——'

'Mother Angelica,' Justin said quietly but quite compellingly, 'would you allow me to handle this on my own?'

The nun hesitated, then she went out and closed the door behind her.

'Justin,' Lucy said, 'don't think——'

'I'm not.'

'You don't know what I was going to say!' she objected after a moment.

'Was it along the lines of—don't think I'm coming back to you after what I overheard this morning?'

Lucy took a breath then sat down on the bed. 'Well, yes,' she said baldly, and added, 'If you must know, I was highly embarrassed this morning. How did you find me so quickly anyway?' she said exasperatedly.

'I remembered what you said about Mother Angelica once. I thought you might have—turned to her. But why embarrassed?' he queried.

'Because... because I felt as if I'd never left school, for one thing!' She subjected him to an indignant pansy-blue gaze.

'Some of the things you heard this morning are true, though, Lucy.'

She turned away, picked up a blouse and started to fold it on her lap. 'I know, I do know,' she said suddenly. 'I... it was one of the reasons I married you. I didn't know where else to turn, I didn't have the maturity to stand on my own, and now look at me: back here,' she said, barely audibly and with a rueful look around.

He smiled drily. 'With two people who love you nearly coming to blows over you this morning.'

Her eyes widened. 'She *wouldn't!*'

'She certainly looked as if she would have dearly loved to flatten me when I introduced myself.'

'Well—but that doesn't change things.'

'It does for me,' he said. 'That—and finding that you'd left me.'

'What do you mean?' Lucy whispered, and her heart started to beat erratically. 'Look, I have to tell you, I saw you and Joanna in the paper, holding hands! But in any case, since he nearly died—Tim—things have been different, and they were never quite right in the *first* place so—I couldn't help knowing you were thinking of what might have been. After all, you were the one she turned to. Then——' her voice cracked '—then this morning I had to listen to all those things you said about responsibility and vulnerability and innocence as if I were your *ward*, not your wife. How can you expect me to believe I'm really anything else to you, Justin?'

'I don't,' he said, 'not yet. But I'd like the opportunity to explain. Will you let me try to do that, Lucy?'

'H-how?' she stammered.

He grimaced. 'For one thing, not here. Will you come away with me now?'

'What if it doesn't——' she stopped to brush away a tear '—make sense to me?'

'Then I'll do whatever you want me to do—bring you back here, if you like.'

She hesitated. 'Well I have to warn you I'm no longer a pushover, Justin. Nor am I a broken flower.'

He was silent, just watching her as she sat straight-backed on the bed, her chin tilted although her eyes were still wet, and there were tired faint blue shadows beneath them. Then he moved as if to ease some mental burden and said, 'You never were, Lucy. Should we perhaps—get some breakfast? It's about that time.'

'Not if you live here; I've had breakfast *and* a round of rounders,' she said with a sudden faint smile, though sobering almost immediately.

'Coffee, then?' he suggested.

'All...all right, but...' She gestured almost futilely.

'I'd better make it good,' he said with a sudden touch of humour.

Lucy caught her breath, but said bravely, 'Yes.'

CHAPTER TEN

JUSTIN drove her to the Rocks and chose a restaurant overlooking Circular Quay with an open veranda where they had the Sydney Harbour Bridge almost overhead, the sails of the Opera House rising across the Quay and the waters of the harbour dancing before them in the morning sunlight. And he went inside to place their order, taking quite a few minutes.

Not that Lucy minded; she was trying desperately to get herself together and even wished he'd been away longer when he and the waiter arrived together with orange juice, a pot of coffee and two waffles spread with syrup and heaped with ice-cream.

And she said quite spontaneously, 'Oh, dear! I don't know if I can fit it in.'

'Try,' Justin murmured, sitting down opposite her. 'Look upon it as brunch; that's what I'm doing.'

And they ate in silence for a while until he pushed his plate away and poured the coffee. 'Lucy——'

'Justin . . .'

They spoke together, and he smiled slightly and said, 'Go ahead.'

'No.' She pushed her plate away and wiped her mouth. 'I'm not sure what I was going to say anyway.' She shrugged desolately.

'All right. Lucy, you were right about Joanna—once. When she left me and married Tim, a kind of blackness came over me and I swore I would never forgive her, or him.' He paused and watched her searchingly, 'And, while it *wouldn't* have been true to say it didn't matter whom I married after that, it was not a true marriage that I offered you.'

Lucy closed her eyes then made herself take a sip of coffee. 'Go on,' she said in a gruff little voice.

'But it *was* nevertheless a gesture prompted by all those things that Mother Angelica and I catalogued so embarrassingly for you this morning. In other words, I did care very much about what became of you, not only Dalkeith, and I did know how much Dalkeith meant to you and I did mean to... always have your best interests at heart. Unfortunately——' he paused and stared into the middle distance for a moment then returned his grey gaze to her with something bleak and sombre in it '—certain things happened unexpectedly, as you know, and while I would never have gone out of my way to flourish you at Joanna, when it happened I couldn't help feeling—a certain sense of revenge.'

'Go on,' she whispered.

'But——' He stopped and looked at her white face. 'When I realised that, it very quickly changed to a feeling of remorse and I came very close, when you offered to make our marriage a real one, to letting you go.'

'I wish you had,' she whispered, then her eyes widened. 'Well, you did try, didn't you? That night. I wouldn't take you up, though... oh...'

'Lucy, don't blame yourself for that, blame me,' he said harshly. 'I could have done it if I'd set my mind to it.'

'Why... why didn't you?' she stammered.

His grey eyes held hers. 'Because I found I didn't really want to.'

'So you could go on avenging yourself?'

'No. So I could really have you.'

'But... but why?' She stared at him bewilderedly.

'It had become a matter of growing urgency for me, that's why, Lucy.'

She sat in stunned silence for a moment then said, 'Because you're a man and not a monk sort of thing?'

His lips twisted into a dry little smile. 'You've accused me of that once before. No. Because of *you*. An enchanting, sometimes wayward source of increasing fascination for me in every way, including the most intimate way—that's why I did it.'

'Are you trying to tell me you started to fall in love with me, Justin?' she said with difficulty.

'You've hit the nail on the head, Lucy,' he agreed.

'I don't know if I can believe you...'

'I think you should try.'

'But look here——' she sat up agitatedly '—it didn't stop you treating me like a child sometimes—don't you remember what happened that night in the twelve-mile?'

'Very well, as a matter of fact. May I point out that it didn't stop me from treating you like a woman either?'

Lucy sat back and felt the colour rising from the base of her throat but with an effort, tried to compose her thoughts. 'Well, it didn't blot Joanna out entirely, though, did it?' she said huskily. 'I know because,' she paused, 'for one thing I saw how you and Tim looked at each other after the sale of the Cawnpore filly, and there could be only one reason for you two to feel so hostile towards each other, couldn't there? Joanna,' she said miserably.

'No, it didn't blot out Joanna *immediately*, Lucy,' he said and unexpectedly reached across the table and put his hand over hers. 'But that was partly habit, I suspect, and mostly a sense of remorse towards *her* by then. You see, seeing us together, sensing my frame of mind that day they flew into Riverbend to look at the filly, opened it all up for Joanna again. And I began to wonder if I was some sort of monster, letting her see that flash of revenge so that it all came back to her at the same time as I was falling in love with you.'

'Did she tell you this?' Lucy queried very quietly. 'That it had all opened up for her again?'

'Yes, but not until the day after Tim nearly died.'

'But you knew it was happening to her all the same?'

'Yes, I guessed,' he said and both his voice and eyes were completely sombre. 'The kind of thing that in my black days I'd dreamt of planning, only to find a growing horror when it happened quite unplanned. And I guess most of the hostility I felt towards Tim Madden then was motivated by something you put into words once. How could he put Joanna through it, all over a horse? Which was why I was glad he had to pay so much for it in the end.'

'Oh,' Lucy said on a breath. 'But that still leaves—I mean, you still *cared* about her otherwise...not that I mind, I mean...I don't know what I really mean except that Joanna Madden is very hard to hate,' she said frustratedly. 'And she did turn to you——'

'She didn't,' he said drily. 'Sasha did that without Joanna even knowing, which was just the kind of thoughtless thing Sasha was so prone to doing. Joanna was actually horrified when I turned up at the hospital, horrified and terribly guilty. Because she blamed herself for Tim's heart attack, you see.'

'Why? And if so, why did you stay with her nearly all day?' Lucy whispered.

He moved his fingers on hers. 'I stayed because she *didn't* have anyone else to turn to and once the damage was done, I couldn't stand by and not try to bring some sanity to the situation.' He paused. 'Why did she feel guilty? Because Tim knew what she was going through too, perhaps he'd even deliberately brought her to Riverbend to find out if she'd got over me—I don't know, but I'm quite sure it was his perhaps subconscious shot in *our* war, buying the Cawnpore filly for such a high price. I think he was trying to prove something to Joanna.'

'I see ... oh, yes, I see,' Lucy said, her eyes widening. 'So they were right, his children, after all?' She stared at him with her lips parted.

'Partly right,' Justin agreed grimly. 'What they didn't know was that by then what I felt for Joanna was an affection I probably will always hold but that I was no longer in love with her, and never had been in love with her the way I love you. The other thing they didn't know was that the shock of seeing Tim at death's door had opened Joanna's eyes to her love for him.'

Lucy sat staring at him, absolutely arrested. Then she said shakily, 'Do you really believe that?'

'Yes, I do. In fact, that picture you saw, which I wasn't even aware had been taken until Shirley showed it to me because she'd seen you looking at it with tears in your eyes—that picture was the final chapter. I went to see Tim with Joanna and together we told him all this, but I *only* did it because he'd had a relapse just after I arrived back in Sydney and she was desperate enough to contact me and beg me to do it. I think we got through to him. And I wasn't holding her hand as such; she'd tripped on an uneven tile and I stopped her falling, that's all. We parted outside the hospital.'

'But why—Justin, did you know how Joanna felt the day after Tim's heart attack?'

'Yes.'

'Why didn't you tell me?' Lucy whispered. 'How could you tell Tim and not me?'

'Lucy, when I came back from the hospital the day after Tim's heart attack I wanted nothing more than to do so. But——' he paused and looked deep into her stricken eyes '—you went away from me. You made it quite clear you didn't want to hear any more on the subject. You even looked... repelled by it all. And I thought it was too late, that I'd lost you and I didn't deserve any better because I'd been such a bloody fool for so long. I thought, why would you want to go on being involved with me after all I'd done? I felt, to put it mildly, as guilty as hell as I watched you withdraw further and further from me. Then I saw you and Rob Redding, I saw you laughing again, becoming in his company your old, natural, lovely—it's hard to put it into words—self. And I saw the way he looked at you and I thought... how much better it would be for you to be loved by someone with no dark past, someone young and uncomplicated——'

'Justin,' Lucy broke in urgently, 'yes, I did go away from you, although not because I was repelled but because I couldn't stop thinking about what might have happened if Tim had died, and wanting to die myself out of sheer misery. You see,' she dashed at the tears brimming in her eyes, 'you don't know this but Sasha... Sasha seemed to confirm my worst fears just the night before at the dance.' She told him what Sasha had said and how it had all seemed to add up to the fact that Sasha genuinely believed it wasn't over between him and Joanna. 'Then, when it was Sasha who rang up...' She stopped and the tears fell unchecked now.

'I might have known,' he said grimly, and closed his eyes briefly. 'You were right, why I put up with her I'll never know. But she was wrong.'

'She did apologise for all the things she'd said before,' Lucy said involuntarily.

He looked at her piercingly, 'Such as?'

'Oh, Justin,' Lucy looked away, 'I don't think there's much point—Sasha...was Sasha, I guess.'

'Do you—believe what I've told you this morning, Lucy?'

'I...' She bit her lip and swallowed, wondering if she dared to believe it.

'But there's more,' he said very quietly. 'When I got back to Riverbend and you were gone, when I confronted Mother Angelica and came close to hating a nun of all people because she thought she loved you and understood you more than I did, I knew then I could never let you go, Lucy, even if I believed you'd be better off with someone like Rob Redding. I just—in the end, couldn't do it.'

Lucy stirred. 'This morning you said you'd take me back to the convent if I wanted it.'

'Do you?' he queried quietly. 'I was hoping to persuade you to give me a second chance. I was hoping if I told you all this and told you how you've grown into my heart and life so that I'll be lost and lonely for the rest of it without you, you wouldn't want to. I was hoping to be able to prove to you that we are soulmates.'

But although he looked deep into her eyes, Lucy twisted her hands and said disjointedly, 'I want...Justin, I want to believe you with all my heart but...'

She stopped and became aware of a droning noise overhead, then aware of some of the waiters and some passers-by stopping and looking upwards and starting to smile and gesticulate, so she looked up herself and saw a light plane flying over the harbour bridge flying a banner. A banner that said in high, rather hastily painted letters by the look of it but quite clearly all the same, 'I LOVE YOU, LUCY. JUSTIN'.

She choked, looked upwards incredulously again then turned to him and whispered urgently, 'Justin, is it really true?'

'If you let me, I'll spend the rest of my life proving it to you, my darling Lucy,' he answered, and then she was in his arms and everyone's attention turned to them as it became clear to all and sundry who Justin and Lucy were, and people started to cheer and applaud.

'I think we ought to get out of here,' he said into her hair.

'Oh, yes, please,' she said. 'Oh, no! Do you think it will get into the papers again?'

'I hope it does,' he replied, and added with a grin. 'It would also make my day if Mother Angelica were to see it. Let's go.'

'How did you arrange it?' she asked laughingly as they were ushered into a suite at the Regent very close by.

'When I went to order the waffles. I rang a friend of mine who owns the plane. He gives flying lessons and trails banners and was just about to take-off, fortunately—although I'm afraid he thought I'd gone mad.'

'I should get in touch with Mother Angelica,' Lucy said sobering. 'Actually, I got the surprise of my life when she verbally attacked you this morning, because her advice to me had been to fight for you if I really loved you, you know, Justin.'

'Was it?'

'Yes—that's strange, isn't it?'

'Not so strange if she'd perceived that you do really love me.'

Lucy grimaced. 'I don't think anyone ever doubted that—Justin,' she breathed as he suddenly held her very hard.

'Sorry. I don't know how I could have been such a bloody fool, that's all.'

'Should we...should we go to bed, then?' she suggested. 'It might stop you feeling like that.'

He lifted his head and she caught her breath at the blaze of love she saw in his grey eyes as well as the laughter.

'Did I say something wrong?'

'No. Oh, no. Lucy, another thing you said once was that you'd rather you were married to someone with no experience but who loved you so much it didn't matter—that's how I feel right at the moment. Delighted, devoted, renewed—and dying to go to bed with you.'

'That's lovely,' she said softly, and moved in his arms.

They made love twice before lunch and spent the afternoon in bed recuperating, as Justin put it. They watched a movie on television holding hands but at about four o'clock he went into the adjoining sitting-room and made a couple of phone calls, telling her just to be patient when she asked about it. Half an hour later there was a knock at the door and he brought into the bedroom a large box and a slim envelope.

'What's this?' Lucy asked.

'Open it, the box first.'

So she did and discovered two dozen bikinis inside. 'But——' she stared at the colourful throng dazedly then lifted her eyes to his '—if this is what I think it is, I only need a couple.'

'What do you think it is?'

'The Seychelles?' she hazarded.

'More or less. Open the envelope.'

So she did and this time her eyes nearly fell out of her head. '*Justin* ...'

'What do you think? We've missed the QEII here but we pick her up in Singapore then cruise to the Seychelles, Mombasa, Durban, Capetown, so you could well need more than two bikinis—hey,' he said softly, 'don't cry.' And drew her into his arms.

'I'm not. I mean, I am, but only from happiness. Do you remember saying something to *me* about romantic gestures—well, yours are the very best!'

'Well, my first one wasn't the most original, but perhaps I'm learning,' he commented, and kissed her leisurely. Whereupon they made love once more and then he had dinner and a bottle of champagne sent up.

'I still don't need two dozen,' Lucy remarked with an impish little smile, later.

'I know. I had an ulterior motive there, I'm afraid,' he drawled. 'I ordered them on approval so you could try them all on and select the ones you liked. With my help,' he added gravely.

'Ah,' Lucy murmured then laughed.

He raised a wry eyebrow at her. 'That amuses you?'

'No, it delights me actually, and very shortly I shall do just that, try them all on, but first of all I think I'll do this.' And she leant over and kissed him fleetingly on the mouth. 'Thank you. For everything,' she said a little shyly.

'Lucy——' he caught her wrist then pulled her on to his lap '—God knows I feel guilty enough about you as it is——'

'Justin, don't say that,' she whispered. 'It will make me start to wonder again if——'

'Then let me tell you this,' he said quietly, holding her against him gently. 'I have a vision of my life now that's inextricably linked with yours. I'll always have the memories of the beautiful girl who became a woman in my bed and told me she felt ... translated, and I know I'll want to keep on translating her for the rest of my life. As well as living in love and laughter with her, as well as fathering her children, as well caring for her—and receiving the special sort of sunlight you bring to me, Lucy.' He tilted her chin and stared deep into her eyes. 'There is only one way to say it. I love you, I love your body and your soul and I can't live without you; it's as simple as that ...'

If she had any last doubts they were dispelled the next morning when they went to see Mother Angelica together.

'Ah,' that wise nun said as they stood before her together in the study that hadn't changed for so many years, 'you've resolved it. Mr Waite, I *was* rather hard on you yesterday but one thing in the end convinced me that you loved Lucy and that was the look of inexpressible relief that came into your eyes when I told you she was still here safe with me. God bless you, my dears, and don't you dare have any christenings without me!'

And to Lucy's joy things like that kept happening, little touches of proof. Such as the occasion on their delayed honeymoon aboard the pride of the Cunard Line somewhere in the Indian Ocean between the Seychelles and Mombasa. It was a formal evening and she'd dressed in a strapless midnight-blue evening gown that moulded her figure and had a slit up the front, and put her hair up.

But she had to return to their state room when her tights laddered and it took about twenty minutes to change them and assure herself she was perfectly presented again. When she returned, Justin, looking magnificent in a black dinner suit, was standing with a group of people all superbly groomed, indeed he was flanked by two stunning women who seemed to be vying for his attention. And Lucy's heart missed a beat as she saw, as she approached, the distant, shuttered look on his face, something that had been missing these past few weeks. And when he looked up into her eyes, for a moment his own were moody and disenchanted.

Then they changed and he excused himself briefly and came towards her almost as if he was heading her off.

'Is something wrong?' she whispered.

'Yes. Come outside.' He put a hand on her elbow and steered her out onto the deck, and kept steering her until they reached a secluded area with no one around. 'This.' And he took her in his arms.

'But... but why?' she asked minutes later when she'd been thoroughly and urgently kissed. 'Not that I'm complaining...'

'I missed you,' he said simply. 'I couldn't work out why you were taking so long, particularly as everyone was asking me where my gorgeous, sensational wife was. I wondered if you'd fallen overboard—or found another man.'

'Justin!' she breathed her eyes wide and stunned.

'Moreover, Lucy,' he continued and while his eyes were amused there was something else lurking in their grey depths. 'I need to be reassured.'

Her lips parted. 'How...do you mean right now?'

'Indeed I do, Mrs Waite.'

'Like this?' she said not much later but in the seclusion of their state room, and reached for the zip of her dress.

But he stilled her hand as he stood before her, his dark head inclined, and murmured, 'Just so. May I?'

And he released her hair first and ran his fingers through its golden length and then undressed her item by item until there were only her new tights over brief silk panties. He laid her on the bed and drew them off slowly letting his fingers lie cool and firm on the inside of her thighs until she moved with desire and said his name in a grave, husky little voice.

Then he ripped his own clothes off and lay down beside her and took her with a lack of finesse that he apologised unevenly for, but an unmistakable hunger that told its own tale and took her to heights she'd never reached before.

And in the sweet, drowsy aftermath of their love, she cradled his head to her breasts, and felt herself to be Justin Waite's true partner in all things.

'I don't know what got into me,' he said after a while with her now lying in his arms, as he stroked her hair.

'But when I looked up and saw you coming back at last, so...utterly lovely, I just knew I had to do this very shortly.'

'I'm glad you did,' she said and drew her fingertips down his face. 'If I thought I'd been—translated before, it was nothing to this.'

He laughed quietly and hugged her gently. 'We've missed dinner.'

'It's well lost. I love you.'

'Even after—wrecking you like that?' he said wryly.

'More so, and——' Lucy paused, then sat up and looked down at him wickedly, '—you're also the man who flew a banner over Sydney harbour telling me you loved me, don't forget.'

'The second man—is it any wonder I could get a bit paranoid at times?' he replied lazily, his eyes on her pink-tipped breasts.

'The only man. For me,' she said firmly, and lay down again.

'So you do...believe me now, Lucy?' he said in a different voice as he took her into his arms again.

She turned her face to his and laid her cheek on his chest. 'Yes, Justin. Is it...is it so important to you?'

'The most important thing in the world,' he said very quietly.

'Well, you're the most important thing in the world to me, so it's worked out astonishingly well, in fact.'

'Yes, it has. Thank God, it has.'

HARLEQUIN ✦ PRESENTS®

Introduces a brand-new miniseries from

The Crightons are a family that appears to have
everything—money, position, power and elegance,
but one fateful weekend threatens to destroy it all!

March 1998—THE PERFECT SEDUCTION (#1941)
The Crighton family had been the cause of scandal and
heartache for Bobbie Miller, and she wanted revenge. All she
had to do was seduce Luke Crighton, and the family secrets
would be hers to expose.

April 1998—PERFECT MARRIAGE MATERIAL (#1948)
Tullah was tantalized by her boss, Saul Crighton. A devoted
single father and the sexiest man alive, he was perfect marriage
material. But he plainly didn't see her as the perfect wife!

May 1998—THE PERFECT MATCH? (#1954)
When Chrissie met Guy, she thought her most romantic
fantasies had just come to life. But Chrissie had a family secret
that Guy could surely never forgive....

Available wherever Harlequin books are sold.

Take 4 bestselling love stories FREE

Plus get a FREE surprise gift!

Special Limited-time Offer

Mail to Harlequin Reader Service®

3010 Walden Avenue
P.O. Box 1867
Buffalo, N.Y. 14240-1867

YES! Please send me 4 free Harlequin Presents® novels and my free surprise gift. Then send me 6 brand-new novels every month, which I will receive months before they appear in bookstores. Bill me at the low price of $3.12 each plus 25¢ delivery and applicable sales tax, if any*. That's the complete price and a savings of over 10% off the cover prices—quite a bargain! I understand that accepting the books and gift places me under no obligation ever to buy any books. I can always return a shipment and cancel at any time. Even if I never buy another book from Harlequin, the 4 free books and the surprise gift are mine to keep forever.

106 BPA CE65

Name   (PLEASE PRINT)

Address   Apt. No.

City   State   Zip

This offer is limited to one order per household and not valid to present Harlequin Presents® subscribers. *Terms and prices are subject to change without notice. Sales tax applicable in N.Y.

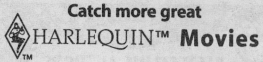 

FIVE STARS
MEAN SUCCESS

If you see the "5 Star Club" flash on a book,
it means we're introducing you to one of our
most STELLAR authors!

Every one of our Harlequin and Silhouette
authors who has sold over 5 MILLION BOOKS
has been selected for our "5 Star Club."

We've created the club so you won't miss
any of our bestsellers. So, each month
we'll be highlighting every original book within
Harlequin and Silhouette written by our
bestselling authors.

NOW THERE'S NO WAY ON EARTH OUR
STARS WON'T BE SEEN!

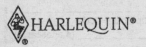